Q. Bagbjört Huang

FOOL'S INFERNOS

FIRST EDITION #1

Q. DAGBJORT HUANGINGTON

Fool's Infernos

Who seeks shall find.

SOPHOCLES OF KOLONOS (GREECE)

Contents

I

Sea swell

From shores to oceans, plateaus to cliffs, mountains to plateaus, will they not stay who they are? Or would it say that a thundercloud's a raincloud?

Skyfall

Copyrighted work, individual authorship—code name Quarter-staff. All rights reserved. Please contact the amanuensis for more information. Wait 3 seconds for the actual file to play.

Look, I didn't even expect things to get out of hand so early in life.

Some people think the world is peaceful now, while others believe it's still unstable. But following the crowd won't make your life easier. There may already be a contaminant in this session, though—but heed the warnings; I don't believe it's anything good.

But please do note that the contaminant is not of physical traits: not skin, face, faith, race, or nationality. It just seems that the substance *is* existent among all of us, no matter who we are or where we are. On the worst sides, I had experienced plenty that would have turned me against the sun to fight for the dark that said it was the actual peace: car crash within Shanghai that cost my mother's life, the time when my stepmother—Yueliming Wang's () mother—temporarily starved her child for 20 days straight with only water as "food" just for the appearance of mere water-based paint splatter on her face, the time following that being the point where she was hit by an high-speed car that was of "punishment" (ended up in the ER when the stepmother was locally defamed by People's Police), and the time before when I was beaten almost to death due to my involvement in supplying Yueliming with the basic *actual* foods, and I could just go on… until my jaws are lost.

The event that I could consider retelling was exactly in 2018, a mainland-based event that, by all means, I would've ended up six feet under with others cheering my death as the mainland in question is not my native country—but just the country that once was allies but now more like frenemies.

And I almost forgot to tell you my name. My name is Quanfei Zhong Huang (), born in 2007 in Shanghai, China, in the Pudong district. I am shortsighted, but I do wear glasses every time I am awake. Han Chinese boy if you want, while Yue is of the Hezhen Chinese.

Now it's time to rewind the year.
,,

The place? California, United States of America—yes, the location of the main Hollywood [land] branch of the American film industry. Don't ever expect the story to start with big names within the state, but for this, it began somewhere within El Dorado County for the location's sake.

To be more time-accurate, though, the point where I could start telling you the story was May 31st—the very last day for the 2017-2018 school year for Yanderolle Middle School, located just on the outskirts of the Folsom-Cordova Unified School District. Relative time is the day's astronomical twilight, 4:32AM.

"Good morning," Yue said as I awoke. "Just stay balanced and take your time."

Yueliming Wang was a female with the same shade of black

hair as me and much more normal eyesight than me. She didn't wear contact lenses, as she had perfect visual acuity. Yue was roughly 5-foot-9 inches tall, while I was more like a half inch taller, though ever since that one court case where our original parent or guardian lost custody of us, she has been in a foldable wheelchair—stuck there so far for roughly *years* to no end.

Don't expect me to be strong either, with a torso that was so thin that it didn't take much pressure to feel the rib cage, spine, and pelvis bone, and a head so worn of wear that for the most part within the scalp, it's completely faceted with dozens of possibly broken pieces.

"Morning." I felt for my glasses.

"Packed your bags?" she asked. "Our *second* stepmother's waiting for us."

Yue and I have had a very strong relationship ever since we became unrelated siblings. Why was it that we seemed to have two stepmothers? We had one, as Li's mother had to have the court case I mentioned earlier after making headlines that would be disgraceful even if it stemmed from her great-grandparent's way of correcting misconduct, which led to our brief time in the orphanage. Since then, I could say that my childhood friend and I were emphatically inseparable, regardless of how far apart we were.

"Yes," I answered, "I packed a life of two weeks abroad inside."

"Good," Yue said. "You forget a lot, but I can remember what you forget."

Since we were on the bunk bed at this moment, I carefully climbed down the ladder and unfolded Yue's wheelchair by the foot of the bed, pushing it over to her side without incident.

"BREAKFAST!" a voice called to us from downstairs. "GET READY!"

That was Mrs. Mayridge, our 30-year-old stepmom, who worked within the microchips industry as one of the few people who innovated the next generations of the employer's products, such as the Z0AX1Y98BNW99235 chip, which provided nine times better performance in every spec than competitors while remaining as an independent unit that was no larger than a thumb. She had a husband, though he died at 20 because of a multi-vehicle crash in which his car was affected on all four sides due to part of three cars performing an illegal road race, and the fourth at the rear was tailgating even though it was to save fuel. She had brown hair with blue eyes, and around this time, she would be more likely to wear pajamas as her work started around two hours after we awoke.

After doing the usual morning routine of brushing our teeth and washing our faces, we went downstairs to eat eggs, bread, goat meat, and have a drink of approximately 1 entire cup of milk. We got into her (and her deceased husband's) 2008 Ford Expedition and drove to school immediately. We reached there in approximately 32 minutes, as the roads were not as congested as in Los Angeles.

"Have a good time," Mrs. Mayridge said.

"Have fun for the summer," I said back.

I came to the rear of my stepmother's Volkswagen and lifted the trunk's door with one hand, pulling out our wheeled suitcases with my other hand, before closing it. With Yue, your everyday wheelchair person, I was the one responsible for the suitcases, as Yue could carry her backpack.

The school was bustling with activity as the end of the school year approached. Although Yue and I didn't have the same classes, we both attended a multi-sectioned school where school subjects were divided into buildings that were at most a 7-

minute walk apart. The only few classes we had with the same teacher within the same time frame were Social Studies, Math, English, and Science.

"So try not to blow things up even though it's the last day of school," our science teacher, Mr. Hay, said. "I don't need another failure."

"Okay," the student in the back said, "Can I eat Cheetos?"

"No," Mr. Hay answered. "The immediate environment must be stable."

One lab table near the same general region immediately put up their science fair poster's cardboard backing towards us, seemingly acting as if they were stripping the poster of its contents.

"Now, try not to do the unsafe things we talked about."

With Yue as my lab partner, I carefully gathered the supplies that were for the class project, or what Mr. Hay calls "the lab". This was a chemistry session, so I did have the necessary materials in the bin, but not the equipment in case of a disaster that resulted in the contamination of those few pieces of equipment—which the rules themselves are partially meant to prevent.

"Now, are you all ready?" Our science teacher asked, "This is the final and 180th day of the year, and I will be retiring next year. This is an exam, so following Californian law, do *not* make explosives, drugs, or hazardous materials. I shall monitor you all as you work and succeed." He plopped down on his chair and pointed to the whiteboard. "Make something explode much more violently than elephant toothpaste while not going against the state."

I carefully gathered the necessary equipment and assisted Yue in putting on the personal protection equipment before actually attempting it without violating Californian law.

"Okay, so let's do carbon, saltpeter, and sulfur," the class bully Mike Solando said right behind me.

"Yeah, more explosive." His lab partner, Wilson Trevicé, nodded and said, "This will be fi—."

"That's gunpowder." I interjected, "Against the law."

"It's under 50 pounds," Wilson argued.

"It's not commercially manufactured or to be used *only* in antique devices or antique firearms." I said, "The United States Bureau of Alcohol, Tobacco, Firearms, and Explosives does not allow it."

"Fine, we'll go on with something else," Mike said. "But watch your back. Coke… and mentos."

"Let's go with something hydraulic." Yue said, "We'd just need an empty plastic bottle."

BOOOF.

A thousand cooked popcorn kernels came raining down on the entire class like an alternate hell. The poster that once stood like a privacy screen between the teacher and those foodies came immediately crashing down thereafter, apparently having six exploded popcorn bags immediately above *eighteen* (or more) Bunsen burners that were supposed to be for flasks.

"Out, you two." Mr. Hay scolded, "No food in class."

The two backseaters left immediately.

Yue fetched an empty 500-milliliter water bottle from the recycling bin solely meant for bottles and cans. In a few moments, we had just two separate flasks of such to explode relatively non-violently, which included ingredients for a safe elephant toothpaste, a classic Diet Coke eruption, a volcano experiment, and just a bit of the rocket experiment—cork plugging the opening alongside the bottle cap. Other than the cork, we divided the substances into two groups for starters, since this was very much our first time to try to do so.

We first poured in the one containing the vinegar, then quickly poured in the other, unfortunately putting on the cork so fast that there was this big pocket of air directly underneath the cork.

"I got this," Yue said. "Hui, anchor it in the case."

I clasped the bottle with both hands and held it firmly as if it were going to rocket off onto the roof. In mere seconds of the twist, I didn't expect it to be off like a gunshot, piercing a hole in the ceiling so violently that the hole was approximately twice as wide in diameter as the actual projectile itself. We were the first to pass, albeit in the category of making a paint bomb, as I and Yue used a few drops of almost every food coloring to differentiate between the flasks.

Due to that damn cork that we placed too fast, our science class earned a free temporary permit to use the showers. You could've seen the photo of Yue and me in the *Notable Occurrences* section in the school's digital newspaper, pretty much with the teacher himself leading the way in case the mixture was too dangerous to leave alone.

"Quanfei and Yue…" Mr. Hay said as he got out of the showers, "You earned an A-plus."

"Hey, Quanfei," the maintenance guy walked up to me, "Is this yours?"

He handed me the bottle cap that had been in our experiment. The bottle cap was totally fine, but what wasn't was the cork, which was stuck to the bottom of it like someone brutally forced it against its will, though a bit soggy from the substances used.

Three classes later, it was math—without further incident, though, in terms of position; I sat the one up front and closest to the door while Yue sat right beside me as every other desk from hers in terms of rows joined with the one before—thus forming something in an arrangement for pair-and-shares year-round. After another class, which was just PE, I was in English class, though I shared the next and very last class with the bully.

"Hi, Mr. Palmflower." I greeted my teacher the moment I entered the class.

"Morning." Mr. Palmflower looked over the newspaper and said, "I hope you're having an awesome day."

"Yue!" Garcia exclaimed. "It's the last day of school!"

Who was Garcia suddenly? As I fully remember, she was this Spanish-Mexican girl who was regular for her age in terms of height, with dark brown hair that derived like mixing paint from her parents, and eyes the color of jade. Anyone who isn't her friend, parent(s), or teacher doesn't want to mess with her, as she can get badly physical like a delinquent. With a dream of what she wanted to be if she survived through the school years, she wanted to be a researcher in biology, stepping toward that goal through small but seemingly unrelated part-time jobs such as working in fast food restaurants or working as a local lifeguard, each paying about a basic double-digit salary per hour above the minimum wage.

"Yeah," Yue waved, "don't ask me for sleepovers."

"You technically have a sleepover with your friend." Garcia herself smiled and said, "That one who reads entire textbooks."

"Yes," Yue commented as she shifted into her seat.

"Hey bro," a voice behind me said, "last time we'll see."

That was Fred. I don't know his last name, but out of all four of us, he's the jock, I'm the nerd of social studies, Li's the one who is a human calculator, and Garcia was the one who would excel in biological sciences. Popular as the football type, he never wants to cheat on Garcia, as he only knows how to tackle someone who can definitely aim for his phallus.

"Long time, then." I turned to face Fred and said, "See you on the other end of electronic waves, whether they come out offline. Till we meet again."

We did the handshake, and as Fred and Garcia's seats were on the exact opposite end of the row, we had quite some distance as suitcases lined up and piled up just outside of the door for a slightly easier load-in to the tour bus that was our eventual ride.

Before anyone could say anything further than that, the late bell for classes rang. Since we barely had anything to do, Mr. Palmflower allowed us some free time until the bus arrived. At that moment, I looked around the class and found the class bully's seat empty, like there was nothing there other than the typical seat and desk.

"So, have you all packed your bags?" Garcia asked as I and Yue came over.

"Yes, we have." I replied, "I didn't bring a textbook, at least."

"Come on, man!" Fred joked, "Pack until it's full like a freaking balloon!"

"The heavier the suitcase per person weighs, the more jet fuel the Boeing has to take, and once at its limit, it can't take anymore, and the owners of those have to go on a separate flight. We do not need another flight that does the J-curve."

"Okay." Garcia leaned a bit closer to Fred and said, "This would be my first ever flight."

15 minutes later, the bus that was chartered to carry us to the airport arrived, and then the entire half-hour drive All the way to the airport, we had no trouble since of the absence of the bully of my grade level, and so far, I do not know where he had

even gone. The airport was in Sacramento, with the Federal Aviation Administration's location identifier being SMF.

Since my school normally lasts 8 hours for a single regular non-minimum day, fast forward to 1:44 PM, and we arrive at the destination. The same old Sacramento International I had known of since 6 years ago—the same routes, the same road signs, the same general layout—and we were flying with United Airlines on a Boeing triple seven-dash 200.

Around 1:54 PM, my gut feeling foreshadowed that day as I and others lined up at the gates while the plane stood at the loading zone. The entire, or almost entire, terminal branch was decorated with United Airlines' logo.

The interior was expectant, as if like a flying bus, albeit divided by the sole I-owe-you the world has now as the universal exchange unit. Business class seating was up and at the front, while economy was near the rear, and I don't know what premium class was for within the airline services—situated right between economy and business. Four rows of overhead storage bins were all functional at least, with random seats being filled in first, like the airline just didn't care about the efficiency of getting in.

Yue and I sat in D and E thirty of the seating arrangements, though, with Fred particularly sitting in G 31 while Garcia sat in F 31. They stowed the carry-on bags and the wheelchair overhead. Also, they spaced each passenger boarding bridge out evenly to avoid wing-to-wing collisions.

"We'll see our home again in two weeks, alright?" Yue said to me, "This will be all right."

"Yes, I have flown before as a passenger," I muttered.

A moment later, the airplane itself had a pushback, and within minutes, it taxied to the runway for takeoff. V1 speed was then reached a while later, and it lifted off mere seconds later, following a heading of 89 degrees once fully clear of the terra firma.

We reached the cruising altitude of Flight Level 431 in terms of how many feet above average sea level we were. This was the service ceiling of the model, and with a track heading meant for an approach to the District of Columbia from the relative north, I was completely fine, as almost all places other than military bases were restricted to protect the leader, like the classic childhood game in which one would try to get at least one person behind the "guard".

"Hey," Fred tapped me on the shoulder, "yesterday's news came up just now again."

"What is it?" I asked my friend, "Something peculiar?"

"Yeah, some unidentified unmanned flying object was detected, but as of the video, can you just approximate how fast it's going?"

Fred handed over his iPhone XS, and on the Reuters news network's article of the day, I noticed it was something related to flight, but not like a crash or anything, as the headline read:

UFO SPOTTED OVER AMERICA'S EAST COAST

To summarize what I immediately read, the article was completely in the format of the news network—nothing strange there, but as it was blabbering about the witnesses' answers to their questions, I could picture a strange sight, much a bit too paranormal, as the article described an aircraft with these specifications:

1. The plane is as ghostly white as clouds.

2. They reckoned the wingspan to be a margin wider than the Antonov An-225.
3. A twin propulsion system in pairs with a blended-body airframe
4. Only one vertical stabilizer
5. Low-delta anhedral wing with cropped tips
6. Sawtooth-edged weapons bay doors.
7. Capable of Mach 24, as confirmed by two journalists (one stationed in Maine, the other stationed in Florida)
8. Undetectable to the radar
9. An unidentified flying object that changes every single visual documenting medium, such as photos, to something else.

What annoyed me about the article was the last bullet point. It stressed to the readers that we can visually document any object without changing, and this thing in the skies was a strange case of some sort of memory-related entity. The same article additionally said that it was in some sort of holding pattern within the range of eyes upon the coastlines, just never making landfall other than releasing a swarm of flying drones that carried the anomalous trait of electric power loss for those within the visual horizon, as if the mothership herself had enough of it.

Even the video near the headline dividend had changed by the time I merely looked at it, like it had self-destructed and been replaced with some streamer's video of a modded Grand Theft Auto V—failing miserably while doing the challenge.

"Sorry," I said to Fred, "I can't tell as the video's off-topic."

"Dear passengers," the intercom announced, "we are slightly having a hiccup, so please bear with us; we are..."

The lights that were on flickered off, and pretty much everything was in pitch darkness as even the screens in front of us went offline. As soon as that happened, though, something like a 5-kilogram avian ingested itself into the starboard engine. The screens in front of us went offline, leaving us in pitch darkness. Shortly after, an unidentified flying entity weighing around 5 kilograms ingested fuel into the starboard engine. This was the final multi-path crossing point in time, as the 777-200 was a twin-engine aircraft. With the starboard engine going up in flames, we were left with just enough force to maintain a climb, let alone a dive. Not everything explodes when there's fire, and the other engine ingested the same entity that destroyed the starboard engine.

In the seconds after, another drone shredded the roof much like an Aloha Airlines incident, going all the way from the point where the cabin met the cockpit, and since we were already in a dive, it almost decapitated the heads of those at the rear, more or less that it tore off two sides like how one would flip a page, and sure, we were soon left to the elements as soon as the aft pressure bulkhead was torn, much ado about the stowed luggage as they relatively began to almost fly.

"AAAAA..." Yue (or was it everyone else?) screamed as we almost approached the G-forces for red-out.

Me screaming? I might as well want to lose my head for it, but being no fan of roller coasters, I had to, even with the chaos of people almost always doing themselves first, like a mix of the *Hunger Games* and *Lord of the Flies*. I was not so sure we would survive.

The Boeing was never in one piece like pieces of a jigsaw puzzle, though, but it was like China Airlines 611, every square inch from the region where the unmanned, unidentified flying object impact occurred, and I could still remember the details as it broke up like a Prince Rupert's drop.

I was one of the few who got torn off the plane with the seat alone still strapped, so I was just one of the unlucky few who was to be the debris, tumbling uncontrollably as I knew jumping was not an option, as it is to think jumping would even get me off the damn seat. The last moment I was consciously alive was approximately when I was facing downwards towards the ground, going at an acceleration roughly equivalent to a penny, going fast then slow repeatedly downwards, increasing speed as the belly or backside to earth did barely anything better than the entire seat itself, housing much of the mass that had absolutely no such wings to fly rather than to dive.

The cold was too much, and in mere seconds after falling, I blacked out.

Dusk

I could have even died.
    But, as if some force had no mind.
    I survived.
Internally, I rewind
But externally, nothing whined.
"You are alive..." my childhood friend said.
Well I wish I was dead.
Not because of her but of the cold—
Molding itself into what reminded me of the past.
Days that lasts
With unendurable vastness
Even though I was past this
"Place is called Camp." Sun Wukong affirmed,
A place of safe haven,
Not of reapers
Nor of peepers.
That was normal.
Four survived.
Never abnormal.
But when the sundown came...

De Equus

"What in the world?" Fred muttered as we went outside of our apartment.

"What?" I asked, "Something's up?"

"There's a horse on the other side of the apartment," Garcia answered.

"How is that strange?" I asked them, "There's a rider on—"

"It is riderless." Fred interjected, "Normally this would be in a stable, but it has all the horse gear equipped."

"How?" Yue asked Fred, "It's a wandering rouge?"

"No, no, it seemed to be a rogue when Garcia and I spotted it from the patio."

"Since seeing is believing…" Garcia pointed over the roof and said, "You should make two consecutive turns at the nearest pair of crossroads, and it should be big enough to be seen."

"We'll be waiting here." Fred gestured to the ground immediately to the side of our apartment's entrance.

No more than a mere three minutes later, Yue and I saw what Garcia and Fred had seen.

In the early morning, at around 5:30 AM, the road was entirely bare of anything other than the horse itself, trotting seemingly unguided in our direction. The horse itself was as tall as your everyday Shire mare, with features that favored more speed and endurance over harsh terrain than just showcasing its looks.

As if it were my instinct to not startle the horse, I immediately focused my eyes on the forehead as it slowed to a stop. Yue was probably afraid to get any closer, but I knew time was ticking.

"Don't look directly into its eyes." I whispered as softly as I could, "This particular horse takes it as a predator."

"How do you know?" Yue asked in a hushed tone, "You've never witnessed or done a tutorial."

"Gut instinct." I said, "Just wait by the side of the road. We're in its blind spot. This may be evil in a package."

I then slowly waved my arms and hands as wide as possible, making the least noise possible, as the most critical fear may be the fear of something that seems to not even exist.

The horse tensed up a bit but started to inch towards me, somehow in an exhausted manner.

"Hey." I spoke to it. "It's all right."

It whined a bit, but quite quickly started to strafe my position. It'll not be dangerous to go near." I let that trail off.

I immediately began to slowly but not threateningly walk towards it, showing both of my hands and my pockets that I had nothing. By that time, the horse did not have the same edgy look as before but was more or less shifting to a relaxed body language.

The moment the horse came close to my right hand, which was extended yet relaxed, I didn't expect gasps from the neighbors that a first-timer had successfully managed to do something. Duh, I did.

"That is the thousand-li horse." An elderly man said as he walked, "Too swift to be mounted by any mortal man and the only member of its group,"

It whinnied and sort of pawed the ground in response to the elder's question.

Stroking it along the ridge made it calm down a bit, just enough that the horse approached Yue all by itself without further assistance.

"Then, could you tell if it's a stallion?" I asked the elder, who came out.

"It's a mare, by the looks of it," he answered.

"Hey there," a Camp resident around the same age as me said while passing by on a bike, "Good morning."

"Morning." I said as I casually stroked the forehead, "I'm just a first-timer here."

The reaction I received was, as expected, normal. As she noticed the massive horse through her rearview mirror, she asked, "How did you not die?"

"I don't know; this may be a horse with gigantism." I replied, "Don't speak so loudly to it."

"This… only gods can choose who to ride it!" she softly said, "Otherwise, it brings death to anyone else who rides it. Oh, I'd better tell the camp's only news network."

"Wait!" I shouted, but she swiftly disappeared once she made a hard turn left around the corner.

By the time it was 7:00 AM, almost every city dweller had heard about my first-ever feat. According to the timetable that was found on the nightstand, even the school had no one doubting the rumor as I rode the horse to school and left its reins tied up to a bicycle rack. It was front page evening news by the time I left the campus, with every adult around knowing my name and my feat but not knowing my personality as well as Yue did.

But *during* school time?

I was the epitome of failure for almost all activities, as Camp's school is more or less a giant campus only with homerooms, while the classes themselves conventionally took place as a bit of a hands-on method of learning modeled after an intensive, long 9-hour day schedule.

PE was more of an active boot camp for basic training, though, with dull-edged blades that were moderately sharp yet pristine of any blemishes. The Weapons 101 class was guided by Chiyou himself—the six-armed and four-eyed warlord who was more or less at the top of his class back in the day.

"You seem to combine historical European treatises in your style." Chiyou walked by me as I flipped over the training variant of the yanmaodao and slammed the pommel onto the dummy's head. "That's the German death blow, albeit reserved for long swords, not sabers."

"Yeah, I am more of a bookworm."

"Then try a spear. I would recommend it." Chiyou tossed a spear and said, "Not bad for a sword, though."

In the immediate minutes that followed, I guess Chiyou hadn't, as I did suck at even using it properly. One look over at Yue, and she was fine with the small, portable, and rather light weaponry of the ancient Chinese arsenal: swallow tail knives (), throwing darts (), throwing axes (), flying needles (), willow leaf knives, and biao xings (), though the latter gets confused with the Japanese shurikens.

"STUDENTS!" Chiyou roared over the chatter of others, "Field time!"

In a moment, all four of us—Fred, Garcia, Yue, and I—found ourselves not too far from each other, though categorized as either sword, spear, or ranged. Spears were entirely in one group, but swords and ranged classes were in smaller units, so a swordsman who wields a single-edged sword couldn't go with the training of another swordsman who has a double-edged—nor could sabers train with daggers.

Rigor was the component of drilling the proper weapons combat training of the respective weapons to their fullest potential—with no breaks until 15 minutes before class was over, outside in Sector Seven's stadium. The instructor arranged rows and columns of students, including myself, which made it impossible for us to make contact during the synchronous copycat movements.

"Don't put too much stress on your arms," advised Chiyou, shaking my left arm to show me that it should be kept loose. "If you overexert yourself, you'll end up with just strength and no finesse.". The balance between your swings is also good, with not too many wide sweeps."

Please do note that this training was with actual yet blunted weaponry, which meant that even if it was blunt, the first day's curriculum was harsh as an sandstorm. Anyone who had no experience with the weapons the class gave out but had the myth of the media… they didn't fare well in the mid-class test of knowledge for the god of weaponry to see where everyone's at.

That meant no swings so wide that the swordsmen spun like in most movies, no backhanded grips, and several other key tropes related.

Right after Weapons 101 had ended, Garcia, Fred, Yue, and I moved on to various other classes as individuals so that we could at least get more classes tried out in a single day.

I performed well on various basic school subjects such as Math, but what differed from any regular schools was that they were teaching practical modern-day survival necessities such as economics at such an early stage in school life, with basic courses somehow functioning like the fictional SCP-5094's way of teaching with teachers either being gods, demons, or with substitutes, former students of the same class.

"Are there any grade levels in this middle school?" I asked the English teacher who just was the Baize lion.

No, do not think the Baize lion does have a mane, as the teacher in question looks like a Bengal tiger at first glance, though a sharp horn that protrudes like a rhinoceros' primary horn is what differentiates it from the rest of the specimen that mortals sometimes see or personify their characters as.

The Baize lion swished her tail and, without hesitation, replied, "There are no grade levels, or are there grades like in school based on performance? But the closest we get is like a binary of either good or bad behavior and participation points."

The next class I attended was in metalworking, where we had actual hands-on work with every single naturally occurring metal, such as bronze. Entire forges were already set up and lined up in rows, and no two rows were the same as they alternated between copper, bronze, iron, silver, and gold—every one of them having a conveyor belt that disposed of those metals upon request of any user. They included anvils as part of the standardized rule for forges within Camp, as well as all the tools necessary.

"Okay class, never go too hard with the bellows." Ao Qin said, "Don't ever stick your hands into it."

Who was Ao Qin? He is the sea lord for the southern quarters of the Earth, while his three other brothers rule the rest. The god himself was, like many other gods, a shapeshifter who didn't obey the mortal's comprehension of reality. He was wearing proper personal protection gear during his duty as a teacher, so I had no worries that he wasn't a madman.

"Sir, you need fire." Ao Qin bent over at my workstation with some random dude as my partner.

That moment was when I immediately understood why I was here in the first place I simply splayed my right hand into the wood stack within and was about to get a matchstick with my left when I somehow summoned flames like my dominant hand had suddenly turned to a flamethrower, my guts somewhat pulling as if I had a cramp somewhere along the appendix.

The flames roared to life, brighter than a light bulb, and it was as bright as six bonfires combined, so I had to flip down the visor my hard hat was equipped with, though at least I was working with iron in my first metalworking class.

"Wow…" I left Ao Qin quite surprised: "This reached a typical common Ancient Chinese blacksmith furnace's brightness."

My non-powered physical abilities as I went through the classes did involve navigation, though, with some pretty accurate guesses for the Geography class' free time spent on geo-guessing as a competition between classmates—even the places I've never been before, I guessed them with an error range up to 16 yards off the answers.

"Quanfei and Yue and Fred and Garcia of Sector Eight's apartments," the speakers on those stand-alone telephone poles blared out right after school ended, "This is not a disciplinary reminder, but please come to Sun Wukong's office."

A short while later, we were where we were commanded to be, just sitting on those seats, and as Sun Wukong silently finished his banana, we all just sat there in silence, even as the light flickered a bit.

"You all are demigods." Sun Wukong started, "Your other parents contacted me, and I can tell who your other father or mother is."

Out of the blue? Like, seriously, instead of telling us the moment we could remember, we had to wait more than 7 entire years just to get the names of our parents? One tiny fragment of me felt rage, but I knew it was wrong to burst out at someone who couldn't die. Anger is never the answer, though I did have memories of corporal punishment back then—parents would go do whatever they liked in terms of punishment to the extent of abusing their relative position within their families so much that death is an option for them to hand out, though the *prevention* of such conflicts with Confucianism as the school of thought makes it clear that parents have the freedom to choose whichever disciplinary action to take on their child—meaning that the previous generation can inflict what their parents did to them on the present generation and it can go on like dominoes in a never-ending line.

"What?" Garcia said, "I thought they would only exist in fiction."

"The god of engineering, Erlang Shen, was the son of the Jade Emperor's sister and a commoner of the Chinese social structure on Earth." Sun Wukong pointed out, "He used to be a demigod, but now he's a god with an actual task at hand. Even though you, Garcia Sáez, look Spanish, you just have a father who mixes in Mexican blood in place of her actual lineage—Chuang-Mu's being exact, while Fred's the son of Zhongli Quan."

"Okay, we all don't know our fathers." Yue said, "I used to live in a single-mother household."

"Yueliming Wang." Sun Wukong flipped his quarterstaff. "You're the daughter of Ao Guang and something a bit off topic... The medical bay is ready."

Initially, I didn't know exactly what Sun Wukong meant, but he made it obvious when I reminded myself that Yue wasn't acting about being stuck in a wheelchair.

"Quanfei, you're the forge, with Zhurong as your father." the monkey king said, "Would you like to accompany your, um, friend as the medics restore her mobility?"

I turned to Yue just to confirm, and I still remember the radiant smile she had when I agreed to accompany her, though the entire operation was precisely meant to restore her legs without botching it in the process.

The second day for me ended at 10:45 PM, with Yue now fully mobile and happy with us being roommates, not relying on a wheelchair anymore. But what might've been the wood and the last branch to the figurative campfire was the dream I had that very night.

.

The dream began in the same place where I slept. Every little detail, such as the spatial coloration, was correct, but it just seemed odd that there was a hole in the immediate closest wall of my room. It was in full color, though, and without the depth that normal three-dimensional objects have, it looked like nobody cared about how thick the wall should be to support such a high-rise residential building.

Out of curiosity, I stepped closer to it, moving out of my bed, and since the wall in question was up against the headboard of the bed, I stepped through—the entire dream world feeling like it was real, though I knew it wasn't, as in the real world, I was peacefully sleeping.

CLUNK.

I fully stepped through that paper-thin hole, and I ended up just right in some sort of library, though I can't tell whether it was as the hall seemingly continued forever, with bookshelves taller than me, reaching for the skies, and in such a cramped space—the corridors were just barely wide enough for my fists to touch when my arms were fully extended.

A painting that was painted with ink appeared to the left as I went to take a left turn on the crossroads, and it was more or less the traditional painting, so I almost ignored it if not for the text arranged in the traditional reading format of right to left, top to bottom. Translated to English and formatted to modern-day standards, it read:

Xiliang Queen's Decree, Horse Challenge
Written in 2000 CE by the scribe of the 143rd queen of the Kingdom
of Xiliang (1934–2006),

Active 2: The dear Camp's residents have already been informed by the alternate list, which was carefully planned since the fall of the Qing Dynasty, that six entities will head that only Sun Yang of the Spring and Autumn periods in China had ridden for years. The last time we ever had a man enter was a Buddhist monk named Tang Sanzang, albeit he was a stern believer in collecting those scripts back to China in the Tang dynasty. For my only daughter, I firmly believe that no man should set foot in this place since we have a river that we can drink to impregnate ourselves with.

May it be that way for centuries since that moment when a demon seized its chance to run away with him for its flesh may have been granting immortality to anyone who eats it, but for once, I will only allow a special permit to those six—whoever they are—to enter the city for a lifetime.

The horse that is faster than a thoroughbred is indeed too swift unless the gods that they are to ride it decree or list them whenever and however far they would like it—though we can describe it in the modern realm as just pure chance. But conditions apply to those who succeed.

By our codes, there must be no false claims of being the Messengers, and thus, one of the six must ride the horse directly to the market square in front of the steps to the palace. If there are any males, they must not sexually harass or begin to do so anywhere within the city, and all six don't get permanent discounts as do all other customers of markets due in part to the equality clause of the law. Since it's rare to even have someone ride this horse, every misdemeanor committed by any of them will be treated as if it were ten times worse.

DO NOT READ THE NEXT PORTION.

I have now sent the horse to Camp, the hot spot for any half-mortals to prove themselves and reach their potential, and may we release it every night. It must be that way for the horse to get exercise and not clog the streets. In the daylight, may it be only in a special compartment in any of the stables on any given day, but with the horse in a completely different stable every single day on completely random routes. May one of the penghous forget it. It'll be all right as long as one of the future six finds it and brings it back to this city.

The picture that accompanied it was a chest-up portrait of the queen that was next in line.

Then an entire display of more than two thousand pages appeared right next to the painting, and it seemed a little dark in nature, as even though it was from the Second World War by the slang terms used, it was talking about a war in camp over the very horse, like an object that gives one the ultimate powers over everyone else.

As I went down the display, the individual pages covered all 2194 days of the Second World War, starting on the same day World War II started. At first, the diary entries are completely civilian, like how a noncombatant would write them, but then they become more and more madmanic as time goes on, notably from a mere ally or friend who told the diarist of the qianlima—the seemingly asexual species that had only one offspring every generation.

Only a week had to pass for the writer of the diary to go in like a borderline madman. A. Single. Week—no less, no more.

Two weeks later, it was more like a conspiracy theorist, forming a group that, by the unholy religion, was hell-bent on getting its hands on the horse, though it took three weeks to at least get ten members, six to get to just a hundred members, and twelve to even reach the thousandth member milestone.

If ever the pattern repeated itself, then the number of people in the sect would've been a million if not for someone being a rat in the entire system to notify Camp of the very underground operations that were brewing on the 84th day, which was the second turning point in his written life.

From that day forward, the writer's self-psychology became increasingly deranged. A quarter of the way to the end, the diarist began to slowly descend into writing random words on paper, making more and more grammatical mistakes for every following sentence. In doing so, I found that the writer began to forget spacing by the week after.

Two weeks later within the diary, though, the mystery person began to write in random languages for every word, losing fine motor skills, randomizing stroke lengths, and finally, at the very last two pages, a splatter of dried blood, ending with the words:

.

FIND THAT HORSE

The dream just ended abruptly, like power was cut off in an instant, leaving me with just inky blackness like an octopus had squirted from behind the curtain.

II

Sky Flowers

*What was the who, who was the where, where is the
how in this muddle of time crossing with space?*

Bandtone

"My horse... my horse... my kingdom... for a horse." Garcia rested on one arm.

This conversation took place at around 5:00 AM, breakfast time, in the lobby of a neighboring condo. The sun didn't exactly rise, but it was within the typical Nevada sunlight hours and in conditions similar to daybreak. We were eating the typical breakfast, though without cereal, as the Camp did not provide any.

Crowds were a few, as this was early morning, but all were quite peaceful—one guy sipping his black coffee, another woman just reading the news while having waffles—just the peaceful normal that I had needed for the conversation.

"Yeah, your horse..." Fred sipped his glass of warm milk and said, "It needs to be returned as soon as possible. I'll go question Sun Wukong about that... decree."

"Right, but in the dream, it doesn't give us the location of the Xiliang," I stated. "The texts don't say it."

"Well, we could ask the headmaster of Camp to at least pinpoint us in the general direction." Garcia herself finished her soft-boiled egg, saying, "By which means, I might be just simply delivering the horseback instead of going flip-a-doodle."

"Show US!" a new voice shouted right behind me.

Instantly, I felt a slight silvery metal brushing against my throat, and I raised my hands in surrender to whoever threatened me in such a way. No one stood up for me, but the occupants immediately went down to their knees in case I was killed out of greed, and the bloodshed continued.

Unplanned, but they caught us off guard.

"SHOW US THE MAP!" The blade of something—whatever it was—moved up my neck a bit.

There was no time to ask why, as in such situations, no criminal would answer questions all day. With a glance to the sides, I could identify who the perpetrator was, though it was one guy that was behind Yue.

"OR ELSE!" the same guy threatened with a tighter grip on the chest, "This mole rat working for the scum dies!"

The potential murderer did stress that out by moving it to the side, where he could easily stab my neck.

Garcia was the first to slowly rise, though with an air of being on her bad side. No one else dared to, but as the criminal seethed in anger, he mistakenly shouted, "YOU— STAND DOWN! I GOTTA RIFLE!"

"Through your [BLEEP]?" Garcia snapped.

That did roast the criminal to the point that flex tape can't fix a comeback.

Fred slowly began to inch sideways, with the one who committed such a misdemeanor confused, as if it hit him with a flash grenade. I could tell that the male was trying to make a comeback, but it would be awhile before he threw away his weapon and threatened us with death by head twisting.

That was when Yue grabbed his arm by the shoulder, and with one forward step out of her chair, she made him bend forward as I immediately moved out of the way.

"Are you sure?" Yue asked the man in his ear, "You shouldn't mess with the one I like."

"Okay, okay—ow, ow, ow." The apparent 18-year-old winced in pain.

"Never again." Yue didn't release the one in pain. "You'll see your stone unmarked on any GPS."

The police went barging into the room where we were and, without any sort of guns, placed a flying guillotine over his head and carried him off. The object you may ask about is a portable head-slicer that conventionally doubles as a bag for the severed head, with the blades easily triggered through a mere light tug of the rope trailing from the top of the device.

"Sorry that I couldn't defend myself." I began.

"No, it's all right." Yue gave me a light peck on the cheek and said, "I might've confessed too early in public."

"Yeah, but we make mistakes." I turned to face Garcia and said, "You kind of roasted me."

"Sorry, I didn't mean to." Garcia suppressed her laughter. "I was aiming for the guy to stop shouting."

"Let's go back just to check if our stuff is secure." I said with a slight smile, "Sometimes, such events as this can be a deception."

In the immediate minutes of opening the door to our rooms, there was nothing stranger than our bedrooms being almost a haunted space. No other areas within our condo were as strange, though, and as I do still remember, the bedroom that Yue and I shared as roommates had on one side a lump beneath the bed strangely shaped as if a bag was underneath, while the other was—visually normal, but when I pressed down repeatedly along the length of the bed, I found just one multi-function pen—the type that had two sliding switches for the option of being a brush or ballpoint. I did another round of the same process and found a custom wristband—the kind that *looked* like silicone but consisted of a tear-resistant, solid, opaque layer smooth as marble filled with a non-Newtonian liquid. When I merely positioned myself in any sort of defensive brace position however, it transformed into an circular and silvery 3-foot wide shield entirely made out of Bin steel— the kind that *looked* like Damascus steel, but has an infamous hardiness to not even budge in the forges anywhere among the mortal's technological knowledge while having some greater level of fear-induction than the Aegis at an additional cost that it would be phosphorescent.

"Why is this messenger bag here?" Yue turned over the blanket on her end and said, "There's no one who could get inside here."

I then opened the side drawers that came with the same bed, finding nothing else other than two pieces of paper, both fortunately written in English in the format of a letter. The looks of it recently placed both of the sheets, though my eyes drifted to the very end of the letters written—the place where I expected some name that I knew as a mortal.

But neither of them had any. It might as well be a trap, as I remembered much of the history of the four major wars that had enemies setting such things to harm their foes.

"Yue, come and see this," I said.

"What?" Yue walked over and said, "There's a trap?"

"No, but two letters, completely written but without the closing."

In a moment, we were sort of figuring out the first four of the six "W's" in reading the letters, which were: why, what, when, and where... but the hows and the whos still remained blank.

"We could see more if we looked into the messenger bag," Yue huffed. "There is a chance that those two could be in it."

Unzipping the bag, we were left surprised that it had no absolute bottom, but as if the insides were painted in the blackest black or some sort of omnipotent developer never bothered with the interior collision physics, it seemed endless. Yue herself was the first to reach into the very mag, as one letter explained that it was hers given from the person, though it might as well be her father or his other two sons as the third son died in the hands of Nezha.

"Just an sheng biao?" Yue pulled out a entire 1340-foot long rope with an 7-pound dart on the end. "I thought it would be a fisherman's anchor."

"You excel at such weaponry, y'know." I said, "I suck at spears and any weapon that requires both hands."

I pulled down the slider that would push out the brush-tip endpoint around the same moment I used my other hand's thumb to pop the cap. Within the same time frame that it takes a human eye to blink, it elongated and expanded, its materials transmuting into a pufengdao that was crafted with seven sheets of the highest-quality metals that were for mostly extreme cases of melee warfare: the carbonado spine was pinched by two titanium plates, which also assisted in rooting the blade to the carbon steel hilt, while much of the blade was of the same material as my shield.

I read the paper that was addressed to me, and in the small print footnotes area of the backside, one of them exactly read:

CAUTION: MADE FROM THE FOUR SWORDS OF ZHUXIAN JAINZHEN, THE IMMORTAL KILLING ARRAY—THE WRISTBAND IS THE ONLY ANTI TO THE EFFECT

When I got to the last bit of the sentence, I went almost defensive about my weapon's ability as I remembered the legend of such a thing—a trap that can kill gods and mortals alike without any modifications. The dilemma here then was, if it is so powerful as to not quite be the one-hit killing trap it used to be, then it might as well be the McGuffin of the timeline, but with a trade-off that, despite having one-hit obliteration, it didn't have any elemental prowess nor any memetic effects rather than having a secondary written trait of returning every single time the one gifted the weapon is to be disarmed in combat—same goes with the wristband, which I put on my left wrist.

I didn't trust that letter due to an unverified sender, so I moved to the living room and tried basic attacks at varying speeds, from a snapping motion to a moderate sweep, progressing through all sword stances before I was sure that it wasn't a burden when I needed it.

I took it with a grain of salt that this particular anomaly was named the dragon's eye saber by the letter, though it did inform me that the other slider would produce a yanchidao (goose wing saber) when pulled down like normal, with a tap from the cap of the very pen making it shrink in its inactive state; if it is not capped after tapping, then it would behave like any multi-function pen with an endless amount of ink.

"Lucky you." Yue said, "I get a sheng biao for long range, but in close-quarters combat, I have just a kunwujian."

"Don't destroy the objects." I capped my sword and said, "These seem to be ordinary though, but did you read your letter that some dude sent?"

"Yes, I did—but to avoid another potential civil war, let's return the horse," Yue said.

Then some sort of burglary alarm blared, and the TV nearby

suddenly went live, displaying a collage-like live streaming video of some library, though when I scanned one of the screens, it was happening *now* at Camp's Library.

"THREAT IS HIGH," an automated voice echoed through the streets. "ANYONE INSIDE, PLEASE STAND DOWN."

That very robbery was committed by an autonomous entity, so to speak. I don't even know their identities at the time of the crime, but it all started out as if they were ordinary civilians visiting the center of knowledge. Those hooded gang members were like teens with some light issues; they were hooded and masked so that their identity couldn't really be given away, though with different gloves, they stood out.

The CCTV cameras didn't record sound but motion, though, as what happened when the short-looking thief asked one to get a book on a high shelf turned for the worse, beginning with the very same criminal drawing out the earliest weapon one could call a manually-operated machine gun—consisting of a crossbow, slot, and lever—and in the case of the event, they were solid bronze.

The action itself technically falls under killing a noncombatant, though the other two did something similar and proceeded to "shoplift" the books. No one stood up against the crime; they just let it happen. No one *made* it stop.

Even when physically covered from head to toe with identical clothing items that covered their bodies so that no easy identification could be made with the ones who saw them, no one even challenged their morale.

"Two crimes in one day." Yue muttered, "Now this is not good. Why are they doing the exact repeat of the Qin dynasty but leveling up a notch?"

I took note of that and observed closely as it happened in real time. No fantasy books were burned, but they took all other books that would even be useful to the tiniest degree off the shelves. With the help of two partisans of such an event, they carted those same kinds of books, dumped them on the steps of the library, and deterred any civilian from even acting against their purpose.

"You SHALL NOT!" the person shouted repeatedly to anyone who walked over.

In a moment, they set the books that fell down the steps alight, much like the Qin dynasty's way of trying to limit political philosophies to just legalism.

"The aliens must go!" the entire gang chanted aloud as soon as they finished.

They all weren't referring to the little gray men that sci-fi sometimes displays, but in the political sense—us and myriads of others. Yue and I had looked through the same topic before we even had Camp as our home, and I can tell you: no one needs bloodshed.

Hate pretty much only generates loops with no end. If any nation were to ever go full-blown Great Leap Forward with a government-held version of the insane Cultural Revolution, the first step is already setting more into the dilemma of how much freedom versus control one can have for others—and with this situation, the ransom item's probably going to be the flippin' horse as the thieves ringed the burning pile.

Once the police captured them, though, the baddies went like a mad dog or a horse with rabies, if that's even close to a description. Most of them managed to escape, though in a short moment, one policeman died and one felon escaped.

With the cameras switching to the main walls, the thief managed to escape without any valuables other than the clothes the sinner had on during the crime. Nobody chased after the human, though it made the middle finger back at Camp before it was too far away to be seen clearly.

The TV automatically turned off after that.

"I never knew..." Yue said, "People may be good or evil."

Garcia soon turned up in our room.

"Is everything all right?" Garcia asked, "My godmother packed us enough supplies."

"We're okay." I said, "The news of such an unforgivable crime."

"Yeah, even though Fred is born on American soil but with a Chinese godparent..." Garcia said, "We should probably go now."

"Who would be riding the horse while others..." I soon forgot what I was about to say.

"We'll switch every day." Garcia beckoned us to come: "We must go off-roading with the same horse."

"Let's go at random." Yue said, "Within every twelve hours, there must not be two consecutive three-hour periods with the same rider, with the last rider of the horse not allowed to go first the immediate three hours after."

"Would that be a bit too predictable?" I said, "If we have that... but on the other hand, we could have random spans, with each three intervals so-and-so."

"And then let the horse choose which it wants to ride first." Garcia added, "We don't want an angry horse."

"You've got a point," Yue said as she slung the bag over her shoulders.

"Come on, Fred's waiting for us." Garcia beckoned, "He has already contacted Sun Wukong about the whereabouts of the Xiliang nation—it's going to be a cross-country hike to the Atlantic front."

"Then we're ready." I put my pen into my right back pocket and wrote, "Call-up Indigo Zebra."

Thornbit

The first day out of Camp, and just... chaos happens the next.

According to Frank, we would need to travel along a linear path that went from the 36-Northern parallel to the 37-Northern parallel. The particular thing was that we had already moved an entire 96 miles with the horse itself hitched to a wagon full of, let's just say, boxes for the current queen from the Monkey King, as we couldn't see what was inside of them due to the labels.

To almost pinpoint accuracy, I would say that we already crossed the Nevada-California border into the infamous Death Valley—the desert is pretty infamous for high heat and being flat as a playa.

Don't picture it as a desert like the Sahara in Africa, but it was more like Arizona, with more than 1000 plant species, a tad bit more than 50 unique plants, a bit more than 300 species of birds, 3 species of amphibians, 36 species of reptiles, and five species of fish—though it's highly unlikely that the biodiversity can support even a small town of humans due to the climate.

"Break tent." Garcia huffed as she looked beyond the place we slept: "New day, new path."

Begrudgingly, I and Fred broke camp, leaving no sign of

former civilization behind—packing everything, such as the single tent we had, onto the wagon.

"I'll be in the wagon." Fred said to Yue, "Quan, could you survey the area?"

I did without hesitation, walking all over for any sign that we missed something that may throw our enemies into the tracks and risk such an enemy that we don't want to split the single knot with. Three times around, I walked, and for the fourth time, I'd say I had found just something.

It all began as a tornado-like sequence of events, just beginning with a slight ruffling of my clothes against the usual wind but slowly becoming more oriented to blow northwest. As for my mental self, I visualized them initially going three miles an hour but exponentially going up to 50—which happened when I turned my head from a ground-looking position to scanning the horizon.

Four degrees westerly of my relative northwest, there was just this ever-growing dust devil—full of rock particles that are quite smaller than a human eye but deadly to begin with— swirling in a whirlwind without any possible jet engines or such nearby creating the effect.

And it was particularly strange as it made a beeline towards our position. Even from my place, where I immediately drew out my pen, the relative bearing didn't change. Even if I didn't have the book that described Sun Wukong's encounter with such a thing, I remembered what it just might be.

"A natural-looking dust devil is out and approaching." I announced, "Position may be spotted."

35 miles an hour straight was its top speed, going as far as to be the equivalent of a tornado having wind speeds up to 200 miles an hour in such a small diameter. It did spin clockwise,

but we didn't want to waste our moment—our single chance— to make it out alive without burning the wagon.

"Go, go!" Garcia, upon the driver's side of the wagon, snapped the whip and said, "Let's go already!"

Maybe I was too stunned to act, or maybe I was too bothered by the choices I could make, but as the rest sped off like bats out of hell, I was the one who was left alone to face the music. The rest left, leaving me with no other stuff other than my weapons of warfare.

Running would likely make me vulnerable, as the other may have more endurance in races than I do, and so, when the dust whirl finally came within a stone's throw, it began to circle, going for my backside, and for some reason, I could sense that it was angry equally as strong as the level of a human.

"Yellow Wind Demon, hear your plea." I tried to dampen my fearful tone of voice by saying, "I plead innocent, though I am of Sun Wukong's city."

"You have traveled down this path far too long." It replied like a human, "Killed once in the past, but the Great God of all things wants you dead."

"Bargain then, Tiger Vanguard."

That was when I just squinted and managed to halt my heart rate, though I was just barely able to as long as I didn't make myself shout.

"Bring back the horse to Camp, and you'll be spared," the whirlwind demanded.

"You say death to us all, and I say… peace."

I could feel it suddenly arming up its potential charge, and just when the wind stopped going in a relatively northerly circle, I immediately summoned my pufengdao. It must've seen it before I did, as it immediately charged at a top speed of 73 miles an hour, which I counteracted with my shield raised almost above my eyes.

The blinding dust slammed against it, and I detected a vaguely humanoid form just almost breaking his concentration to surround itself in the dust devil. Backing off, it then tried to wear away my shield through some powerful sandstorm through its conch-like mouthpiece, blowing deadly silicates my way, but I stood firm, silently guarding my eyes as sand flew past my own legs like a flash-flooding dry riverbed.

"You're using your master's tool of blinding… nice." I taunted, "You wanna mess with water?"

"Fine, then." the Tiger Vanguard instantaneously stopped his whirlwind and dual-wielded twin shuandaos from one scabbard to his right.

His speed was a bit faster this time, with an peak speed of roughly three-thousand miles an hour over 0.4 seconds of time made it figuratively impossible from a complete standstill.

But I guess my godfather Zhurong was more of a god of the high temperatures, and with my skin just somehow pinpointing the source of the irregularity, I managed to dodge not through much wit like at the last moment, but sidestepping at the same time of turning my shield against the Tiger Vanguard—playing it defensively as to fell an giant spirit.

"You little…" the Tiger Vanguard swooshed by.

The sword that was the first to enter within my reach was the left one, followed by the right which turned and struck my shield as hard as the minion could do. Even though my opponent was finitely as buff as [BLEEP], it wasn't the portrayal of strength like most media does—it just that it is a mater of tactical real-time decisions that make an outcome with little time to spare in fights unlike some games where it's turn-based.

The next attack was definitely supposedly an shield-breaker, but instead of swords, the demon kicked the shield like an battering ram, though I was a bit sickened by the mere sound as I myself don't even want to be an surgeon.

The same demon, however, was irritated and an stoic on killing me, going half as fast now with an broken foot even though by this point, it was two minutes into the fight.

"Mortal, you're just make-believe." he said, and charged now with sabers at ready.

I parried the right shuandao, and disarmed his left hand's saber, using no shields this time. We were now momentarily equal, if not for my enemy picking up the other saber in a blink of an eye.

"You skinny-wit." it taunted, "Only one year of training, and I have just so much more."

It slashed in parallel like an saber-tooth tiger's maw closing on its prey, but turning my body such that my chest was perpendicular and in the middle, it missed just by a inch of space. My first slash in the battle was immediately afterwards, opening an wound that was across the chest.

The demon winced and backed off with no dialogue, and hissed as the wound didn't even close. An fire within me probably sparked my anger at this point, but still playing mostly defensively as offensively in the situation would lead to blindness before death.

I slowly closed in on my opponent, shield at ready and my senses alert of my blind spots. The tiger vanguard once again attacked with an slash aimed to decapitate me, but this time, it was not so much of an losing streak as even playing it defensively can lead to my own death—there must be some synchronicity.

"You'll not win for this… one strike."

The shuandao shattered the moment it touched my own pufengdao, breaking away with now an half-bladed weapon. His next move was of that it sent me flying backwards with an single punch at my stomach.

I guess he was an cornered animal.

"Never will I back down." I replied just as it began to resume his own ferocious attacks, "I serve the bright."

Now down to seven-eighteenths of his speed, it was relatively blurry yet more so visible. I parried the next strike to the east, stabbed the demon in the northwesterly position of mine, before it tried to headbutt me as I brought down two mare strikes in the same time frame. It was only when he went full hands-to-weapon combat, was he even sane enough to break his knuckles upon mys shield before making him momentarily look like an narwhal.

With it dropping like an rag-doll, I watched as it began to dissolve like table salt on water, slowly but surely turning to sand through any means possible before disappearing. Even the blood that soaked both my tools faded away, leaving nothing behind.

I already knew I was going to be alone for the second time, but no wagon trails were left behind, not even a note. There is no absolute way to tell north from south or east from west. Neither of us had phones, so I had to rely on my wits to survive.

I could just lay down and wait all day until the sun sets, but it might as well be when they find my bones.

"Well, this is great." I said to myself, "No bones to pick on them, I guess."

I began walking, though I did not know how far I'd go before I had to rest.Reflecting on when I talked to Fred about where the city was, he did tell me that the city was in Virginia, though in some abandoned ghost town called Lignite.

My brain immediately registered that fact, and like I had a perfect internal GPS, I faced east and estimated that it was about 2050 miles away—at least 34 days of a pure 15-hour walk if I was ever to be a mortal who hadn't seen all this insanity so far.

Even though I had been starved more than once for an entire meal before, a human like myself can only survive at most without any known safe environment-based food or water for up to 21 days—and I hope that within 756 miles of where I killed that demon, my friends would be stationed, as any further would result in death through what could be equally considered famine.

I had no absolute worry that I would die by the 8th day or so from my traumatic experience, though I decided that I would walk or run as moderately slowly as possible without stopping other than to sleep since my endurance is not like that of a regular horse.

We'll make it before we know it. one side whispered *You don't want to be starved.*

Six hours later, I was still walking, right around noon, and yet there was no sign of those friends. I was pretty much used to it, though, since it's much better than getting stuck in a dark room for an hour back when I was roughly 6 years old.

"Well, expect the worst of this nice world," I said to myself. "There'll eventually be no one there to help."

Two hours after that point, there were still no one, but one side of my inner self was getting a bit edgy as it was roughly the equivalent of the 1950s classic parent's highly chosen way of punishment—still being carried out as far as 2010 had gone for me.

Eat lunch. one side of me said, *It's already past high noon.*

We don't have any food. the other replied.

Then I could just wait for an hour.

An hour later, the side that was of the past revolted against my present side, screaming incessantly like a child while my present tried to mute what was basically immutable. Don't even expect the common self vs. someone else conflict to happen, but I would rather suffer than live in the same situation.

For another six hours, I sort of internally checked my conditions every now and then, but they weren't as good as they should be. I did totally run on an empty stomach by the third hour, and my legs were somewhat showing signs of fatigue to the point that, by the fifth hour, I was simply a walking, silent automaton.

SLEEEEEEEEEEP... the other side of me was pretty hoarse.

Just stop it, I thought; *we'll die if we don't.*

Those two sides immediately zipped their mouths, leaving me in silence.

True, it was already night, with the sun long gone from the horizon and the moon not in its high position like at midnight.

"You can eat this," a voice right behind me said.

I turned around almost instantly.

Just standing there 10 feet away from me was a figure resembling my childhood friend, with the same proportions as what I had known. A dozen or so alarm bells rang within me as I saw that he was wearing a t-shirt with jeans—dead in the night as if it didn't bother her, though as I recall from the past, it was never like that, with the real Yue wearing long sleeves given any season around the same time of day.

Plus, the entity was holding acorn bread, which Yue and I had never had, even at Camp.

"This bread," the figure beckoned, "is not poisoned."

For a moment, the bread she held flickered to momentarily reveal it was lead covered with arsenic, which triggered my internal alarms as neither was even related to the composition of a natural acorn or to the fact that all of my friends were ditching me in case it was a malevolent entity. Plus, its smell was in relation to some of the deadliest fungi as well as molds—more like old bread, if you will.

"You are, I say." I managed, "Why are you suddenly here?"

"Fred and Garcia ditched me." Yue's doppelganger said, "That beast of gluttony."

"Why this close?" I said, "I won the fight against the Tiger Vanguard."

"The fool who left me is you." the voice changed for a second—a second too long.

The entity's appearance changed in a flash—from a normal living being to a form that would not even exist to move as it lacked all human parts other than the bones and lubricants. Not even glowing eyes; it was more like phosphorus bones, as they glowed just bright enough to barely be seen by the naked eye.

Bearing no weapons, I already knew it was going to be fists, palms, knees, or feet that would strike. Or it could just disassemble itself and chuck 'em.

The first move was initiated by the white bone demon (also known as the Baigujing), which moved as fast as possible for humans without neural limits to the side in a strafing maneuver while keeping its distance. I stood in a ready position, though I kept my left hand on guard in case it decided to attack to my left, and I kept turning to face the demon.

"You're the deer that is to a bear." the baigujing taunted, "A deer that has nowhere else to go."

I drew out my goose-wing saber and just readied myself for a deception maneuver.

The maneuver in itself came, with it suddenly changing in the opposite direction for 90 degrees in relative bearing, going forty-five degrees in the original direction, and then just feinting a charge, ever coming closer with every mock charge and halving it until it went in the same direction all the way relatively south, and I happened to act like I was tensing up for an attack during the whole time it was to my northwest.

"You think you can fool a war nerd?" I spat back, "Even if you fall from the skies, you'll still be it."

I managed to sweep higher this time, though it struck straight through the skull rather very messily like how a poorly-made porcelain pot behaves when a cat manages to push it off any high surfaces. This one demon, in canon, could not go toe-to-toe with Sun Wukong as all it took was an single strike and it was finished.

Human bones were the corpse of the demon, unlike many others, which consist of a biologically feasible existence.

*Dang.*I thought, *But why was this overpowered object given to me?*

As if I were still reaching my goal of going to the ghost town of Lignite, I somehow managed to move forward another 157 miles before sleepiness overtook my will to just go forward like a car running out of gas in the middle of nowhere.

Turncoat's Delight

"**L**ife is never going to be a straight road till hell freezes over," Garcia stated.

I was back with them, all in one piece. This was the third day we were on the path, though, with our position being somewhere east of Ella Mountain according to Yue's and my internal GPS. We were a bit more than a week away from ever reaching the Xiliang Nation's capital, though, still in this brutal arid climate region where only about two entire states away was the infamous Tornado Alley.

This was breakfast time, and we were discussing our journey so far, with the fire pit stamped out and the horse just grazing nearby. Lucky for us, we had to rely on three separate sets of self-contained individual rations, with all of them containing *and* meeting the following:

1. If the ration has allergens, dietary restrictions, or religious taboos, it is labeled for precaution.
2. Must be 6 parts grains, 5 parts fruit, 3 parts dairy, 5.5 parts meat, and 9.5 parts veggies, but with some omissions or adjustments if an ration is for the person that fits the condition of Rule 1.
3. Must not contain any other ingredients other than the

ones listed in rules five to nine, and therefore, those rules must be treated as rule number three.

4. Must be vacuum-packed, freeze-dried, pascalized, and PEF-treated—but for dairy, they must also be pasteurized.
5. Contains cabbage, sweet potatoes, carrots, tofu, or pumpkins as vegetables.
6. Contains rice, cornmeal, or oats as whole grains.
7. Contain either eggs or cottage cheese as dairy.
8. Contains apples, yellow lemons, cherries, oranges, mangoes, strawberries, or purple grapes as fruits.
9. Contains two of the following meats: Alaskan salmon, tilapia, or chicken.
10. Each ration must contain enough molecular essentials for the person with the highest demand in their diet to live 21 days without further meals in a state of constant high activity.
11. Has chopsticks, a plastic reusable knife, and a reusable spoon.
12. Has a packet of clean water with three times the amount required to reintroduce water into the dehydrated foods.

Because of those regulations, the meals we had might sound disgusting, but go to Germany in 1941 for the Auschwitz-Birkenau Concentration Camp, and you wouldn't even expect the prisoners to be civilians eating such horrid meals 24/7.

"True, and we have sixteen days' worth of the stuff in the sack," I said.

"We'll try to not ditch you." Yue assured me, "We'll go all-in whether or not it's going to be threats or allies."

"But here's one more problem," Fred said as he came around the other side of the wagon. "Wouldn't the nation be confused as to why there's one riding the horse?"

"No," Yue said, "have you forgotten?"

"If six is a deception as a possibility, then the queen might be saying it out of the slip of her tongue. You see, some may get nervous.

"How could it be a slip of the tongue?" Garcia asked, "It was only three days ago that you contacted Sun Wukong."

"I sort of see a split here." I said, "There would be some issues."

"A dream told me so," Fred said. "The queen, who was the previous leader of the nation, told me to go alone and leave them behind."

We all, unfortunately, had no phones, so there was no way to contact Camp without wasting days traveling back.

"She also said to kill extras." Fred said as he cracked his knuckles, "Which means you all…"

Spiders from out of nowhere began to tunnel out of their hiding spots among the immediate few yards—just those big violin-sized octo-pods coming straight from the book that the realm or locale seems to hop out of—just seven of what I would fear to speak.I can't read the lip of those seven, but with those fourteen palps… I could tell you: they were definitely happy as children.

"You turncoat." I quickly set my food down beside Yue and asked, "Who are you in this world?"

The spiders immediately tensed up a bit of their legs, drawing back their abdomen before clicking their mandibles.

"The one who delivers."

Fred wasn't his usual self in terms of personality anymore, and with those spiders all around us, they were not even instinctively willing to bend down for negotiation. Fred whistled and the spiders set themselves up for charging for the last time.

"I'm done with you!" Garcia shouted at Fred, "You think you can go alone?"

"That queen included an award of one trillion American dollars." Fred said, "Oh, I forgot, the moment when I entered high school…"

He stepped with his left foot in front of his right, and below the sleeve was a water-based sticky toe (the version that kids can get without breaking the law). The insignia was of a broken hammer amid thorny vines curling around the frame, and on the bottom, curled around like a cowcatcher on a steam-powered train, were the words:

.

The horse will be mine.

.

Instantaneously, I could tell that the group that I heard in the dream was real. The title of the logo denoted that Fred was a definite spy for the faction that the diarist created to find the horse. Yes,

"You all have failed." Fred smiled—not the warm smile he would give, but one that was so cold that he was probably insane, "Thanks for stranding yourselves here."

I could say the day before they were through thick and thin, but with Garcia particularly disliking men who would brag about stuff such as money and living the high life, and even if the screens tell the others that they spend like whatever they want, the true side may as well be that a huge amount is saved with monthly limits of spending between groceries, charities, property bills, staff paychecks, and such with a financial background of either being in debt or nearing bankruptcy.

"You—stay behind." I ordered, "Watch it barren as you die

with that fear of fame."

"I like the fame I already get." Fred stated, I've already got some."

Fred approached his former girlfriend, and I was the first one to block such an approach.

"Get away." Fred ordered me, "You have no right to be walking among us Americans."

"Garcia is now your ex," I said. "Or do you want to meet the one-hit obliterator?"

This was the moment Fred became physically inhuman, flooding his mind with mad insanity and becoming more like a monster. Before I knew it, I was staring into the thousand dazzling eyes of a demon lord—infamously, book-wise, the technical stepfather to seven human-sized spiders, since his body was entirely like a centipede.

Its eyes were always on the move, however, flashing brilliant light like a disco ball, and being up within point-blank range of the guai—the Chinese term for fictional monsters in general—I had to shut my eyes just to avoid being blinded further.

"Your sword will not harm," it said in a voice almost similar to that of the giant spider of broomsticks.

"Hundred-Eyed Demon Lord," I scolded, "Will it be that you have left your post?"

"How good is it to stretch my legs?" the Hundred-Eyed demon lord said. "Your sword's just a twig."

"You want to see that?" I tossed my pen in its goose-wing saber form to Garcia.

"Every hero's sword breaks," the Hundred-Eyed Demon Lord hissed, "You'll be the one six feet under. Spider Sisters... charge."

Don't even think it was an RPG which is turn-based, as this time, it was no longer training. It was now playing chess at

Mach 10 assuming air temperature was equivalent to a hundred quintillion Kelvins.

Yue took out her roped dart and plunged the tip onto one of the spiders as soon as it rushed close and toppled her, fangs bearing wide enough to swallow the dart itself. She did crack the jaw and broke into the gooey bit, killing one of the many 3-ton spiders we were faced with.

"Stand in opposition?" the centipede demon challenged, "You'll be happy about this."

"Sure," I said, "DEADLY N' FRIED!"

I swung out in a wide arc, just barely missing the maw of one of the spiders leaping directly between us.At the moment when it was just halfway over, I drew back my sword, pulling my arms back like I was going to stab myself in the head. Even though the blade was smooth, that one spider's death… it's classified, but the only thing I can easily tell you is that the spiders' blood were very acidic and blue.

"A…!" One of the five remaining spiders of the battle-zone ingloriously into the earth rather ingloriously.

I looked over at Garcia, now in a mood which you don't want to meet her in at any time of day. Full of regret and rage, she pretty much channeled her feeling to her hysteric strength, moving any of the four remaining spiders like they weighed almost nothing.

"Your friends are mine to see forever." the former Fred stated in mockery.

I was then blinded by his eyes in a sudden twitch of all of the frontal eyes, and trust me, it's like a sun had come down in a nanosecond.

"Watch-out-Quan." Garcia ordered, "Spider incoming."

Yue gutted one of the remaining spiders, twirling the rope

around before slamming the poor arachnid face first into the ground. During the entire scene the death was quick as they only took an minute, and if in the movies, this entire fight might as well be slow as an sloth to make it happen in sixty years.

"You'll be right." I challenged him back, "This will be my last day on earth."

Focusing on only what used to be Fred as my friend, I drowned other distractions out like I put on noise-canceling headphones. With thunder, the demon himself struck first using the head like an ram, though I stabbed the head just in time even if I was blind to the current scene.

"ARIGHT!" the centipede reared and tried to buck me off, but I kept on riding, just rapidly moving my sword up and down as if to saw down logs.

I then used fire to amplify its wound, making my fire hot enough to sear the exoskeleton like an crab.

With the bucking that the centipede had, I held on for dear life, though I was witty enough to ride it like an alligator, even if it tried spinning me out of control.

"Get off!" it repeated, "Get off! Get off!"

In an moment, Garcia came over to where I was, mad that her ex was an demon, mad of the fact that he was an enemy spy, and without an word, cracked all of the centipede's spinal cord, ripped er former ex in half, and proceeded to crack the head open like an eggshell.

I was very sickened of the noise at point blank range, and thus.... I might've puked rainbows that morning.

* * *

"Thanks, Quanfei." Garcia said as we rode the wagon, "That

was great."

"I know," I said from the driver's bench, "We are probably more stable now."

"Should we not stop and continue our journey, eating within the wagon while in motion?" Yue asked us, "With threats just bubbling up around us, we… can't risk a robbery."

"Sure," I said. "It'll make the horse almost tired by the time we travel 160 miles."

"So for every 160 miles, we stop?" Garcia asked as she looked out the back, "How about making the thousand-mile horse canter?"

"That would make it pause at 340-mile intervals." I said, "We initially had 2050 miles from where I defeated the whirlwind demon, and now, since of that, we traveled at a top speed of 12 miles an hour beforehand for one entire day—assuming that you two had to slow down early for me—minus the 180 from 2050, and we have got approximately 5 days before we can count by how many hours we have to walk because an horse can't go more than three days without sleep."

"Let's go then," Yue shrugged. "I can wait five and a half days until we arrive."

For most of that day, we had no such issues with the horse or the axle. As far as I can tell, the endurance is keeping up as well, and the food supply is more than twice what we need.

Things that I could once again describe as anomalous came after high noon as we were finishing the same old meal we had for breakfast, though overlaid with scrambled eggs.

It was initially one human corpse lying down off to the side of the path, but the next few miles ahead were *completely* standing up with another one leaning as if it were in the challenge of getting up. Their skin was dry as plums and wrinkly as raisins, but initially, I had no such thoughts on which artist gave them life. They also stank of dirt and flies, though to the point that barely any of them had any hydration on their immediate surfaces.

"Guys, look, corpses." I said, "By the side of the path."

Suddenly, the two that we just passed instantly hopped one step into the trail we left, and with milky white eyes staring, it began hopping straight towards us, though limited by the other corpse.

"Jiangshi—hopping zombie-vampires." Yue said in alarm, "More to come."

The next batch of the same monsters came almost immediately, with them hopping as soon as we were heard. They were all a minor bane to life, though, as I heard from my great-grandmothers, and sure, they were stiff, but their mouths could have a bite force equivalent to a crocodile.

"HIKE!" I snapped the reins and said, "Hold your loose items!"

Yue and Garcia immediately deployed the tarp that would prevent anything from entering from the back. This was the first time it was deployed for this particular model of the wagon, and I did brace myself for the more rugged ride as it was styled without suspensions or brakes.

In a Fibonacci sequence, as it just seemed to be, more and more jiangshi came chasing after us like we were speeding, though we quickly amassed a thousand before we knew it. All of those corpses were within human limits; none of them were even clean for hygiene, as some had fungus growing upon them.

They were like a hive-mind, though, with each deconflicting from the other; some tried to move faster than the horse, but most of them ended up falling dead due to their speed, hopping along like pawns in chess.

"YA!" I snapped the reins once more and said, "Faster!"

One of the solo zombies tried to jump up on the left side but was unfortunately run over by the rear wheel, followed by five on the opposite side just barely managing to stay on and crawl to me, but due to their immobility in most places, the one that was about to slide off the canvas was tumbled by both of the left wheels, the third getting caught in the front right wheel—truly dead in a matter of seconds.

Nineteen corpses forming a wall in front of us weren't so lucky, as the horse itself wrecked the line that could've stopped any ordinary horse in its tracks. Twenty-four followed, but even when combining their tactics, they messed up at some point.

"Good good." I shouted to the horse amid the bloodbath, "Go on, I'll give you extra time to rest!"

A child's cry could be heard the next moment, and with no time to immediately stop like a car so as not to risk the thousand-li horse being unfriendly for a while, I just braced myself for future court, though what I had expected wasn't a child.

It was roughly a tiger-sized quadrupedal monster that had eyes in the armpits—immediately, I can say it was a yayu—a human-eating kind that one wouldn't want to meet anytime anywhere due to the carnivorous nature. Even with the face of a dragon, it was generally adapted to be as amphibious as possible while retaining some level of speed.

CRUNCH.

In a split second, it was already dead as roadkill, with the wagon having the worst hit as I nearly slipped off the bench off to my right, but it was a miracle that the axle was still intact. By this point, the zombies had decided not to risk chasing after us any longer, like they had had enough of this foolery.

"We just barely made it." Garcia got up from the floor and said, "Go at this speed, I guess."

I looked forward, and the scenery seemed to fly past us, though I could only see 70 degrees of the full scene—the rest were blurry, like going through a tunnel. Air resistance was not strong enough, but I could just feel it like the wind

"How fast are we traveling?" I asked Yue," I can't calculate."

"65 kilometers an hour." Yue said, "Drawing in the bloody rear tarp."

"What?" I asked.

"80 miles an hour now!" Yue shouted back.

"We'll make it in two days!" I shouted over the apparent wind, "I might need to slow it down during mealtimes!"

For a brief moment, we were airborne. I had to grip the edge of the seat, and with a look over the side, I could just get a glimpse of the Colorado River passing by us like a blue stripe of water. The next moment, we were back on the ground, all in one piece, as the horse continued accelerating in a straight line.

"HALT!" I commanded, "SLOW!"

The horse, fortunately, followed my commands and slowed down. Now that we had crossed what I would consider the line dividing the sparse regions from the populated ones, we had to make detours—going off of cities or towns and going as slow as we could through cars.

This was still summertime, with our stopping point being another day away from the location where we were going. Yes, the horse is fabled to be capable of traveling 20833 meters per hour, faster than us, and without proper materials, we would more likely die since the faster one has to go, the earlier the command to turn must be given for it to not crash into whatever is right ahead of them.

"Is anyone alright?" I asked, "No one's hurt?"

"Yes," Yue said, "I'm just bandaging up Garcia since she hit the roof of our wagon."

We ended up traveling 17 miles an hour for the rest of the day, and the horse was just barely tired as it passed through the border between Kansas and Colorado.

"So… crossing the Missouri, Mississippi, and Ohio rivers is up next?" I asked them in the back, "Yue, with your lineage, we may need a solid water bridge."

"I got it, and it's confirmed." Yue replied, "But we get to skip the Missouri River as we are far south of the split."

"How are you guys exactly on the dot?" Garcia asked, "Are there any memory items you remember?"

"No, it's just somehow natural." I said, We can just be described as having a GPS inside of our heads."

Just as soon as I said that, a swarm of quadcopters quickly flew around us at ground level, making as little noise as possible to not startle the horse but being small enough that four could fit snugly into a standard baseball. Our horse stopped right at the moment, though, with thousands of them just scanning with all three of their cameras aimed at the ground, passing through.

"This might not be a good sign." Yue said, "It's scanning everywhere for electricity."

"At least we left our electronics back at Camp." I looked around the massive swarm that we were in.

By the time they all passed us, it was already daybreak, with the sun setting and the moon on the other end above the horizon. Temperatures dropped at the regular pace that I expected them, and Garcia turned on the lantern once it was civil twilight.

"I just can't believe we rocketed our way over the Colorado." I said as I stepped into the wagon, "Who would keep the first watch?"

Garcia raised her hand, though it was possible to repent for the sin of killing her ex.

"You keep watch, then I'll go." I smiled.

That night was probably the most peaceful of them all out of the journey that would take an ordinary 1824 convoy from the Illinois capital to the other end six months to make.

Hill Top

"Sunrise, sundown, high noon, midnight," Garcia grumbled as we made our way to the banks of the Mississippi River.

This was the fourth day of our entire journey, so it was very monotonous, even in the modern age. I was still the driver, though, with Yue sleeping, as there weren't many monsters attacking us, as if the previous day was enough to set them on a cautious plan of attack. Even the Zhujian leopard—a panther-sized anomalous entity that is legendary for roaring despite having a single eye and the ears of an ox—decided to walk beside the horse instead of attacking.

I hopped off the wagon, and with roughly six of my own widest strides away, I estimated the width of the section we had to cross. Since measuring depth was impossible, I assumed the worst for the Mississippi River during the summer months.

"We need about one mile of the width frozen." I announced, "Two miles for the worst."

The Zhujian leopard itself growled as soon as so, and within the massive body of water, it just came that one large serpentine monster similar to the World Snake of the fourth common mythology Phaethon rose just enough for us to cross, though it was more like its midsection arched upwards instead of its head, almost completely blocking the river like a dam during high tides.

"That's the big serpent going for us." I got back onto the driver's bench.

"Rowr?" the leopard asked in confusion.

"Nothing to worry about."

We crossed the makeshift bridge without an issue, and there was no need; it was almost like crossing the Rubicon River halfway around the world—Camp was too far away to support us now, and the only mythical Chinese nation to help us was based in Virginia.

The moment we crossed it and moved 30 miles ahead, however, I had the chills, like something was staring out of nowhere.

I have driven around several cemeteries on our way there; I reminded myself, *It's not like the ghosts were too annoyed or anything.*

"I think we need to switch to night travel." Yue said, "An anomaly nicknamed Black Hole just followed our path."

Taotie.

That was the thing that was giving me the chills.

I turned my head to the rear and, through a tiny silt that was almost directly behind me among the pile of food supplies, I saw what Yue was talking about.

A body-less animal that had only its head was following us, sucking everything around it instantly into its mouth, leaving barren earth in its wake that stretched as wide as it was far from our wagon—meaning that nothing survived by each coming second, destroying most if not all matter despite being the size of a German shepherd—absolutely above the critical mass in which its wide gaping mouth held inky blackness, bending light around it like it was also food.

"Kill it." I slowly turned back and said, "On the surface. We need to go dark after this."

"Okay." Yue said, "This will be great as we do not—"

A single drone flew straight overhead of us in a grayish blur of color, buzzing overhead a few times before striking the taotie head-on, causing some sort of smoke magic to fully engulf it like a net, and with the efficiency equivalent to the work done to pop a balloon, the shroud shrank with the bones crunching like it was subjected to an omnidirectional hydraulic press, the mass increasingly becoming beyond critical mass, yet no black hole formed from the event like it had traveled through a wormhole, leaving no trace of it behind other than the soil and the uprooted fauna.

We had only traveled a couple of miles when Garcia exclaimed, "Look!"

I scanned my surroundings a split second afterward, though I did not expect that there could be such a thing out of place as an infected log that had thousands of fungi-shaped protrusions growing on it, though in an almost sparse pattern like how no two emmental cheese wheel's air-pocket patterns are ever the same. About an inch thick of some sort of living tar was covering the entire log, though, the single branch supporting the fossilized remains of a nightingale-sized bird that had died years ago, the bones strangely clean yet held together by the same weird substance emitting a constant fume smelling like geysers, the substance behaving much like a liquid with almost no viscosity, though it didn't spread like water but stayed in place with an entire extra foot in radius from the edge of the substance consisting of the marble, gold, copper, diamond, and obsidian.

"Anomaly. have we seen this once in a while?" Yue said as she looked over the driver's bench.

The air immediately around it soon was abuzz with something of the sort that was similar to the immediate post-thunderstruck stage during a thunderstorm, but quickly dissipated like the log had expended the last of its total remaining energy—or like the last-place runner trying to beat the second-to-last place runner in a marathon, so to speak.

But what used to be a log slowly turned into some bulbous material that, by itself, slowly moved away from us, leaving the substance in its wake like a paintbrush.

Neither was the dream that night any better than that which happened just days ago.

* * *

The second dream out of this entire recording stage is just as sharp as the one I told earlier, though it starts on a Nebraskan prairie similar to the conditions that stood for centuries between a Viking's arrival to the continent and a sailor who just mistaken it for an unexplored section of India. Insert some sort of monochromatic gray all over, and it's pretty much what I first saw, though, in front of a single weeping willow.

Seven children—around 5 years old—were playing around it in an enteral game of tag, though they never even dared to leave the canopy's shade or go directly in front or back of one another, meaning that they mostly tagged each other with arms stretched out to their sides—with the closest child standing at about two feet from the trunk of the very tree, the furthest stood at about 7.59 feet away. Each of them was different, though, coming from the smallest minority out of each continent, with every other child being a female, though I and a thousand others had gas masks on and stared into the dome that encapsulated the area of which the tree grew.

"Tag, you're it!" a child said to another.

The one who was "it" continued to tag another, but the next one that was supposed to tag someone else reversed and tagged the one before him. It went on in a natural pattern like that—fifty percent of the time reversing while the other was just straight ahead. The footprints they left behind on the grassy field were not linear, though it was more like they had the freedom to move anywhere they wanted.

"I've brought a sword!" the seventh child drew out a butter knife from out of nowhere.

The rest drew out similar items, and with a promise that no one could stab one in the eye or choke them, the game went on, albeit slightly further apart, standing at about 7.6 feet for the furthest one in the harmless game.

"Enjoy THE game," a female endgame voice sounded in my ears. "Enjoy the GAME."

The moment after, the children within were six years old, now armed with literal PVC pipes the length of quarter-staffs, and by the time they were halfway into the same game they played as 5-year-olds, it just took a leaf to touch the children's heads and all hell broke loose.

"Did you make the tree lose its leaves?" one of the female children started.

"No, it was probably them," the male child stated and pointed to the four innermost children. "They shook the tree."

"DID YOU GUYS SHAKE THE TREE?" the same female shouted, "Will YOU PAY US a PENNY?"

"No," the fourth child closest said, "We are just playing the game of tag, right? If I ever had to shake it, it would be this child."

The female pointed to the male, who was the fifth child closest.

"Someone must've shaken it."

They advanced into their 6-year-old form, and now things get pretty ugly as their behavior patterns show edgy distrust. The game of tag went a bit faster, and it was when they were eight… the seventh blinded the eyes of the sixth, which was sprayed with a water gun by the fifth. With the retaliation to the fifth child done by the sixth child, the seventh joined in, progressing to their eight-year-old forms in which they bore the same butter knives except to cut down the very tree.

"I need it for firewood," the seventh stated. "Your use of wood is a waste."

"I do need it for my mansion that I will build." The sixth said to the others, "It's not a waste."

The very argument continued back and forth, bickering and arguing about which one should rightfully cut down what they termed a "forest." By the time they were nine years old, everyone around me outside the dome was just on their phones, though it was nothing short of the events in the world within the dome.

"ENJOY THE GAME." the female voice repeated, "ENJOY THE GAME."

Ten years old, and it was started by the fifth child, who broke the line that had been there for five years, heading silently straight for the tree, and with a hatchet, began chopping down the tree, which the seventh immediately used a literal ice axe to assassinate the fourth; the fifth fortunately had a flash grenade, stunning the remaining living children.

The fourth child notched and released an arrow immediately

to the seventh's neck, with the sixth firing a fork and gouging the eye of the one who killed the seventh Total collapse occurred with each child making a seemingly deeper cut into the tree, and by the final two children, one fired an airsoft gun at the same time as stepping onto a landmine as the other made the final tiny cut required to fell the whole tree.

Almost immediately, carbon *monoxide* began to leak through the tree trunks, gradually filling the dome, and people took notice of that just seconds later. There was no noise but sheer panic as someone tried to take off the mask but caused his death through explosives implanted at the forehead or just suffocating—meaning that the dream world had no oxygen outside of the very dome itself.

Well, once the ground erupted into what looked like a large arena full of the ruins of some building's foundation, it had pure oxygen, and even my gas mask was gone.

We were among the ruins of the former dome, though, built to be much bigger than cameras from inaccessible points filmed us like it was a game show people do enjoy. Instead of humans versus humans, it was more like humans versus machines.

Unfortunately, the types of machines were not the ones meant for civilians, with weaponized parts and heavily armored joints—the form they took was roughly like a human automaton, though armed, as one very rare story said of something much stranger than a walking Pinocchio with the intelligence of a human. It broke Asimov's rules on what defines a robot, as all three laws simply state that a robot can kill another robot under the order of a human but never kill a human.

Positions? They positioned us on the arena floor, along the edges, where the gates behind us were somehow padlocked shut with an invisible barrier, forcing us not to go there. Every other participant except me was a human, with the rest being robots designed to kill anyone. The entire arena was roughly as wide as the Roman Coliseum in its heyday, so that if superimposed over it, the diameter would exactly touch the furthest edges of the property reserved for those games instead of the field within the walls.

"Enjoy THE round," the same female voice announced. "The last one standing wins the argument."

Fast forward mere minutes, and with an entire eight of the stadium blown up with a high-explosive conventional terrorist bomb, I was the last human standing against a machine of my height that was very well my death bringer. The crowd beyond the barrier was completely wiped out, and the last one standing was just two of us: me with my handy one-hit sword with the robot's armor just hanging in chunks, hobbling into the stadium with a flaming foot like a granddad, slowly inching away from that cliff that leads directly into the stormy seas.

"LAST ONE STANDING!" the female voice shouted. "LAST ONE STANDING!"

Pointing my shoulder to the abdomen of the very humanoid, I ran towards it as fast as I could, easily tackling the very android with both arms immediately wrapped around the waist, knocking it clear off the ground before I held onto his other foot and spun the machine as long as I could before releasing it.

The dream shifted for the worse, as I now, as a dream self, found myself exploring wide open roads with so few activities and thousands of "model citizens" looking almost alike in fashion to the point that each one wore the same mask. The same haircut was a mandatory stage there, as I even found one being pelted with stones just because the citizen had an inch too long strand of hair and wasn't wearing the hijab as the citizen in question was a female.

No miniskirts, as the females in the scene never knew the year.

"What's the year?" I asked a male citizen in my dream.

"It is the year 107," the man behind the mask replied, "To our godly leader, Archie."

Confused at the moment, I followed up with the question, "Who invented the hamburger?"

"His grandfather, Alex," he answered as he continued to watch the stoning.

Help! a soft voice of some sort of ghost whispered

I turned, and the crowd began to just leave. The girl's dead body was left as a reminder of what the Chinese used to do for heads of state. The ghost was of the recently dead citizen, just a child that was about 10 years old, just clinging onto sheer existence.

"I'll help." I whispered, "I almost died when I was just barely 7 years old."

Really? the soul whispered, *For real?*

I then mouthed, *Yes, but now... where do you want to go?*

People around here want me to go to hell for not wearing a hijab, even though it's strictly mandatory by law. The girl said, *Though I sometimes wear them in front of government-employed spaces such as police, hospital staff, and others... I just want to go there.*

She pointed straight up at the sky as if there was no limit to how high I could jump.

"The seventh Pleiades?" I asked out of nowhere.

The girl nodded and said, "Remember the story of Harrison Bergeron and Orwellian 1984."

As if a swarm of cranes picked the soul up to the place where she pointed, soaring higher in somewhat of a corkscrew before being picked up by eagles, higher and higher until they couldn't reach the skies. I didn't see her again as my dream faded into bleak darkness.

III

Land-bird

*Flee or fly, they may see, but an gold can be pyrite
made of ice and wood.*

Serpentime

"**N**o men are allowed within the city," a guard at the only gate of the city commanded.

"Halt!" I commanded our horse.

This was the very day we were supposed to complete the decree. In front of me were four guards in total—two on the watchtowers and two by the bridge that spanned the Impregnating River. The city itself was as wide as it was tall, being almost perfectly round and with walls just at the right thickness so that it could both provide shelter from enemies while maximizing population—and I can tell by the back of my hand that the immortal who was told in the well-known story was also there off to my left beside the well that reached down to the river.

"Are you with other men?" the guard herself asked. "If you are, then we'll have the oil ready."

The horse nickered a bit.

"We are here to deliver the queen's wishes." I replied, "I have no other men, though by far—"

"Good," The guard signaled the drawbridge to be lowered, "You, just of a way, while we take them inside."

"Wait, Beth, did you note that this man's horse is one of the few Chinese pegasus variants that your mother sent off?"

"Kate, here's the thing." Beth turned to the other guard and said, "This is a man that deceives us."

"The thousand-li horse, the most prized as we kept the previous name-holder." Kate said as the drawbridge lowered, "This foal was the fastest of its age group, being directly related to the *original* qianlima."

"How is it? You can easily confuse it with a sky horse or tianma."

I didn't participate in the conversation, but already it was getting pretty heated up over those two enemies' thoughts about whether to allow me in. I just simply sat there, waiting for a verdict, even as the portcullis rose.

"What's going on?" Garcia sleepily asked, "Is there something wrong?"

"They're deciding to kill me." I whispered to Garcia, "Since I am a man."

"He doesn't have the papers!" Beth pointed out, "Only the horse!"

"Sure, but do you even expect 10 days' worth of food to fit in with 1000 stacks of paper and medical supplies?"

"You know, we haven't even changed our clothes," Garcia said to Beth.

"THE QUEEN ALLOWS HIM IN!" the one guard at the watchtower to my right shouted.

"Fine," Beth threw up her hands in exasperation, "You're allowed to go."

I then just lightly tugged the reins to make the thousand-li horse start walking.

"With all ado," I said to Kate, "Thanks."

"You're welcome."

The crowd of entire women parted an alley for us to fully walk through almost the immediate moment when the horse's hooves touched the inner city limits, going straight to the central plaza that was quite a distance away.

Every person in the same city had varying body shapes, skin tones, and a mish-mash of colors—the population from just a sample I saw was diverse enough to not cause a biological collapse. With the same sample of the Xiliangs, I deduced that they may not be *homo sapiens sapiens,* but they could be a branch that could still mate with mortals, but with a semi-prevalence of natural muscular builds that were as strong as twenty of the strongest modern men. What was almost universal among them was their height, reaching the limits where ordinary mortals couldn't physically exist but mathematically could through the square-cube law.

To compare them to an entirely different society, I would say they had an absolute blend of the warrior culture of former Sparta, the intellectual levels of the men of Athens, and the hardy will of the Chinese just to survive—which meant that the city was partially basic, surrounding a circular plaza where structures around it did their best to fill in the space.

"This city's nice." I mumbled, "But I have to abide by the order."

"You there?" a voice directly in front of us beckoned.

I turned and immediately straightened my back.

At the steps of the rather medium-sized palace was an 18-year-old woman who was much, much taller than anyone else—an outlier in height among the citizens who were present but within the range where the square-cube law deemed possible. She was wearing her version of an afternoon nap's clothes—meaning that they were locally made of deerskin, while others wore fish skin, goose feathers, and such.

"A man," the queen said out of curiosity, "Two females… where is the fourth?"

"Dead." Garcia said, "Turncoat spy, that was a monster."

"Oh…"

"The horse that was part of the 143rd queen's challenge is right in front of you." I said, "I just haven't used its wings much."

"Servant, fetch me an apple." the queen pointed back up the steps and said, "This is the thousand-mile horse I knew from my childhood."

In a moment, she had an apple in her hands, just leading the horse and the wagon well away from the most congested areas and into what would've been the equivalent of private property as huge bronze gates shut off the public, with the horse following it like a fish to the bait.

"Horsey," the queen said very cheerfully—too cheerful, in fact.

"Um, does it like apples?" I asked the queen.

"Oh, yes, it does." The queen beckoned the horse further into private property.

"We're foreigners, you know?"

"Oh, oh, right?" she said, "You all may be spies on the evil side."

"We just came from Camp."

"Then I must admit, I just like horses." The queen herself finally fully opened up: "My English name's Zolàna Wéʒèkhi Jrmsik."

We followed up by introducing ourselves.

"Garcia, Yue, and Quanfei," Zolàna said under her breath, "interesting. "Could one of you tell me about Camp?"

"Well, they're probably now about to cause another civil war." I said, "We fled because I had ridden the horse without issue and the 143rd queen's—"

"My grandmother." Zolàna interjected, "Go on."

"I answered a challenge I had not known before with the dead person and the three of us going all the way here, though it took several days to not raise any suspicions."

"Oh, what happened back at Camp?"

"First was the horse, then the hostage situation," Yue said as she climbed up to my right.

"Who was the hostage?" Zolàna asked.

The two other girls pointed at me.

"Then there was this anti-foreigner riot."

"Oh," Zolàna backed up into the private stable as we continued talking, "That organization."

"What organization?" Garcia asked.

"It's known as the Order of the Faceless Tripartite," she said. "I don't know their headquarters, but I am your ally."

"Okay."

"It had been an especially boring life during my tenure as Queen, as my mom ruled for 74 years, though she died of illness." Zolàna said as she led the horse to its lot, "This city to me is just a small town that I need to protect as well as balance, but…"

"You want to travel." Yue finished, "Hui and I are both travelers, though just recently, increasing numbers of gains have been on our tails."

"I see your wits." Zolàna gestured for us to come off: "The Xiliang Nation is not a turtle that keeps all body parts tucked in while saying great feats to others as though it can scale a thousand-mile tree faster than a diving falcon."

"So you're expressing your absolute will to leave for Camp?" Garcia asked.

"Yes, even though I have no child of my own, as pregnancy is allowed for all people only above 20 years old and no older than 45, I, by my grandmother's will, can leave once the horse I had seen as a child has arrived here, but I need to deliver a speech first to fish out any [CENSORED]."

We then followed her through the side of the stable, where we went up around four flights of stairs—roughly, with each landing either leading to a room or an entire floor within the palace, with the fourth stairway leading to the floor above the throne room, where, like back at Camp, there was a wide rectangular pillar that blocked direct access to the only balcony.

No signalman was ever to signal the speech as though expected in some children's book, but one after another, the people not too far down below were drawn to the sight as if it were going to be an announcement of emergencies.

"They completed the challenge!" she spoke in her native language.

"What did she say?" Garcia asked Yue, "I am a bilingual person who does not understand this language."

"Quanfei's and my minds can tune to any language," Yue answered over the noise of the crowd. "She just said that the challenge is complete."

Within 5 seconds of the initial cheers, though, my ears picked up several local swear words and boos, and just so happens that mentally, I could see why they'd do it: because she let a *man* in town—not like Garcia or Yue, which were acceptable to them, but I... I may as well be the screamer that is never heard.

"That man's a spy!" one among the crowd shouted almost immediately as soon as Zolàna spoke her second line of the entire speech, "An alien doomed to make us dead!"

I noted that dilemma—the same balance that governs the permits and fences granted to certain persons under the rules set by the people or a leader. Even though in its history, the nation was more like an all-female foothold in the face of a world where early monarchies had no such thrones other than where their husbands died or chose a lonely life path—but in some cases, they overpowered the actual kings that it was similar to being the ventriloquist to his or her puppet.

A unripe green tomato came sailing through the air, aiming straight for Zolàna's face from one of the few market stalls. It was from our relative left, while I was on the right side of Zolàna. Not very good as it was followed by about five or more in slightly different peaks in their flight path.

"Watch out, your Majesty." I shoved her aside.

"Ow." Zolàna winced, "Are you defying—"

SPLAT-SPLOTCH-SPLAT-SPLOTCH.

As expected,k they behaved the way they should be, with their juices just sliding off the surface of my shield, taking a few seeds with them as they gradually slid out.

"Tomato," I said to Zolàna.

"I don't need any protection." Zolàna stated, "I am trained in such things."

About 6 seconds later, a volley of tomatoes, feces, and mushrooms came streaking in, but I blocked them in time for a red-hot iron pike to come whooshing through the air—fully red to the point that the tip was practically almost white.

"Pike at the relative northwest!" Zolàna shouted to me in alarm.

I grabbed it with my bare hands just as soon as it came within reach mid-flight. It was to burn, but it was just one way as I noted of the smell of the brownish stripe: just another common old tactic of making sure that the victim never survives.

The crowd down below tensed up as when Zolàna finally at least got up to her knees before standing, she was not in the jolly mood that anyone wanted her to be in. Physically, she was healthy but was of so much controlled rage that when she pounded the railings, the wedged-in stone leg that was unfortunately directly beneath the shallow depression was completely destroyed, shattering like as if it was an solid stack of flour.

"WHOEVER PLANNED THIS!" Zolàna bu, "Death IT IS!"

"I'll not meddle in Xiliang's politics then," Garcia mumbled.

In a moment, from a nearby blacksmith shop, an entire band of people—all unfaithful members of the Xiliang Nation—were rounded and brought to the bloody chambers, which were deep below the butcher's shop. I only supplied them with the molten iron from the pike that one of them threw, so it was likely they died of their thoughts on the queen, as equally unlikely as breaking free to live another day.

"You deserve the special permit." Zolàna turned towards me and said, "Thanks for that wristband you have."

"Yeah, my father or one of my relatives gifted these two items." I said, "During the journey with that spy of the enemy, I already confronted my fear of famine."

"Why not hunt?" Zolàna asked as we went inside, "The world's big and all."

"This is the United States, which is pretty vague on certain problems such as that every what they call state...," Garcia replied, "does not go against the highest law since 1789 or the document that went along with it, highlighting rights people universally within the nation can have, though those not covered in either are as blurry as hell between states."

"Then do any people out there break the law?"

"Multiple." Yue said, "Each crime has almost always been on the news since 1690."

At that moment, they triggered the horns, sounding in the general direction of the gates. The sound itself was followed by the one-eyed tiger's roar, and it was just time when the earth in front of the gates seemed to suddenly give way to an old layer of rock, each mile it covered breaking the upper layers like it was plowing through like an unrealistic meteor.

By its radius, it was the Mississippi's lake serpent, heading straight as if the previous day's act was just a decoy for the attack to raze this city-state to ruins. Closing in fast at the speeds expected of an active attack, it circled the entire Xiliang Nation once before breaking free and causing panic among the remote Virginians out there.

"It's the same again." Garcia said, "The non-venomous cousin of Jormungandr."

I waited with my own eyes, staring at it, just ready for it to gather enough surveillance data and attack accordingly. I can't tell where it looked, but it was looking for its dinner of the day.

It moved rather inconsistently as it kept going in a corkscrew pattern around the halfway point from the horizon to the city, like how a planet's moon would move if it orbited both the planet's star and the planet itself.

Every single archer among the towers and battlements primed their crossbows or notched their arrows in case a head-on attack was incoming. Every horn blew in a specified pattern. Down below, I could already hear civilians running for shelter or their weapons.

"This will be bad." Yue tensed up. "Since directly attacking would not be wise, but it is."

It just seemed like it was going to execute a siege upon this very city-state.

"Well, down to the bunkers, if your people have one." I

suggested to Zolàna, "Or just pile on the sides of the gates since directly guarding them would not be recommended."

"HALL THE GATES!" Zolàna shouted over the noise, "Be READY!"

An infantry formation immediately consolidated at the gates, clearing a wide corridor roughly the width of the snake at the walls and shrinking down to form some sort of trapezoid-shaped death trap.

For at least several hours, we waited for it to charge, but over four hours, it began to halt like it was running on what it had for breakfast. By the fifth hour, it was transitioning to a more energy-efficient siege maneuver.

"Why… is it not even attacking?" Garcia said, "It should've broken the gates already."

At that moment, it ground to a halt. Motionless, just sitting there in front of its tail.

"Is it asleep?" I asked Garcia, "You're the biologist?"

"I don't know." Garcia said, "Reptiles like this snake are not within my knowledge."

"The first piece of monster dust dropped off." Yue said, "It's dead."

"What?" I asked, "From that far away?"

"Yeah, I think so," Yue said. "Then there's another one!"

I looked closer, and sure enough, it was losing its essence, each piece falling off more and more as the seconds passed. Soon, I didn't even have to squint as large chunks of the same dust broke off, slowly disappearing as if they had a similar reaction to air as with water and salt.

"Who would go with me to the mound?" Garcia asked, "There might be something."

"I'll stay." Yue said, "With Zolàna."

That left me as the only other option.

"It'll be fine." Yue clasped my shoulder and said, "I know you'll always return to me no matter how far apart we are; being the type I am, I don't mind, even though our shared past may seem incompatible."

"Sure then," I said, "I'll join."

Dust-maw

"Quanfei," Garcia said, "Look."

We were upon the massive remains of the Ba serpent, still being blown away like sand in a desert. Most of them behaved like sediments an ordinary beachgoer would expect in a dry season at low tide. To be specific, we were around the 2-mile mark in altitude, along where the spine of the monster could be if its corpse ever behaved like one, and near the front where the skull and spine joined, according to Garcia. The thing that was peculiar about it was another serpentine monster, which was much smaller than the previous, but from the snout to the bottom of the chin, it measured approximately four times longer than the prehistoric *Titanoboa cerrejonensis*, and by the general flow of the body, I figured it was not as massive as the previous monster, albeit its own girth visually was somewhere in the neighborhood of being 22 feet around.

"Be careful." I said, "Maybe a marble rendition."

"Or a living entity."

Squatting down, I carefully removed the dust from the object and slowly made my way through to prevent any attack by the object out of fear of being the predator. Garcia did the same on the other side, and I went extra careful on the eyes, as it would be the equivalent of a lifetime to repaint some marble the size of 16-pound bowling balls made of urethane.

"What's this place?" it asked the moment we were roughly 65 degrees away from both eyes' focal points. "Who are even you humans?"

"We are not in danger." I said, "We just found you in the elephant-swallowing snake."

"Huh?" it was confused, "A faceless guy asked me just to go inside an underwater home the other day… This is not even my bed."

That statement left us both confused.

"Well, you're in safe hands now." I said to the snake, "I'm Quanfei Huang, and that's Garcia Sáez."

"Then what's that city over there?" the snake asked me, "It doesn't look familiar."

"You sound like you have insecurities." Garcia said, "What's wrong?"

"No, no, please, I don't." The snake's tone seemed a bit stressed: "My name's Elizabeth Joanne-Manning."

"Ay, even I have one." I stroked the snake just as it raised its head and said, "We don't want to make you dump the trauma so soon; just spill a bit when you need it. You can speak to us even if we differ from you."

"… daughter of the white serpent." Elizabeth calmed down, "Born on the 25th of December within the year 2005…"

"We'll be going into the city." Garcia said, "Want to come? It's fine if you don't want to since you're the oldest out of three of us."

"Yeah, are your friends going to kill me?" Elisabeth asked.

"No," Garcia said, "It's a city full of Xiliang citizens."

"OK, I am truly in safe hands."

"Want to go?" I asked.

"Yes, I want to, but my death will be in your guys' hands, all right?"

* * *

"You're back." Yue said at the gates, "Who's that?"

"Elizabeth," I answered, "is a teenage ally that was born in 2005."

"Same to you," Elizabeth said.

"I'm Yue Liming Wang." Yue answered, "Nice to meet you."

"You too." Elizabeth had to use the tip of her tail to give a handshake.

Once we were within the gates, people started trickling out. Initially, there were just four or three, but with time, the city had recovered from shock by the time we all reached the edge of the throne room, with Zolàna waiting for us. The females were just unsure whether to attack, laugh at themselves, stage a coup, or break the tradition of giving their freedoms to a single man, even if it is old-school that a man is "superior" to a female, or vice versa, as the two realities may as well end up being unjustified through proper logic.

"Welcome, newcomer to the Xiliang Nation." Zolàna said in a much friendlier tone, "I'm Zolàna."

"My name is Elizabeth," Elizabeth said. "I don't have much memory, but the last thing I remember is sleeping on a bed in an underwater home."

"That's… strange." Zolàna commented, "So to confirm, are you *technically* colorblind?"

"Yes, Your Majesty."

"Quanfei, I have prepared the journey home," Yue said to me.

"Can I tag along?" Elizabeth asked us, "I have never been

92

there."

"Yes," Yue answered, "It's okay."

Inexplicably, the Zhujian leopard decided to walk down the stairs at the exact moment.

"CAT!" Elizabeth freaked out, "It's—"

Her fear took the best of her, and she bolted almost straight out, wrapping around a nearby pole, her reptilian eyes' iris thin as paper, and fixed upon the innocent leopard, who simply passed by harmlessly, sitting down to groom its paw without any intent of actually killing.

"I'm just ailurophobic." Elizabeth stated after a moment, "Don't. Even. Like. Cats. Even-though-I-am-not-allergic-to-them."

The leopard grunted in response.

"Won't you travel in the back then?" Garcia said to the leopard

"You know some Taoist magic, right?" Zolàna asked Elizabeth.

"Yes," Elizabeth promptly answered, "I do."

We stayed in silence like that for however many minutes the leopard sat there.

"Mrowr." it finally got back up to its feet.

"How about we take a break for one day?" I suggested.

"Yeah, we can," Zolàna said.

"Night-night."

Lockjaw

"Good morning." Garcia yawned.

We were still in the city of Xiliang the following day. The same old hustle of the shopkeepers was right outside the palace, and we were in more or less a guest room for visitors such as ambassadors but not tourists.

The room itself was pretty big, though at a minimal space with a floor area for the beds equivalent to three cells of the American Super-Max prison, while the toilet was mostly one of the few where the tank was suspended with a pipe straight down to the bowl, while the shower was more or less similar to how a cement truck's feeding system works except that it sources water from an actual nearby river other than the Impregnating River. Every bed was more or less a slab of marble overlaid with clear white pillows, grayish bed sheets, and green blankets. The nightstands themselves were made of granite slabs with a small depression for a candle to be placed every night, so they were practical as well as somewhat modern, even with a single spiral staircase that led above ground, connecting all the governmental rooms other than the executioner's office.

"Are you guys awake?" Zolàna asked on the other side of the door, "My servants of the cooking division are preparing the meals."

"We just awoke!" I shouted.

I rolled out of bed, but by chance, my reflexes during that very morning weren't too fast, as I prematurely fell and slammed my back onto the floor.

"Are you okay?" Yue asked, "That is roughly a 3-foot drop there."

"Yeah, I am all right." I slowly stood up and said, "Yep, I'm fine."

"Great," Garcia rolled over upon her bed within the city, "Nice alarm you got there, Yue."

"Let's just go up for breakfast." I said, "Nothing to worry about."

"But first, can you get dressed?" Elizabeth said.

"Yes," I replied, "I only have pants, socks, and shoes, so it should be quick and easy."

A moment later, we were in our everyday clothes in the dining hall that was roughly directly below the throne room, with the leftmost wall connected to the kitchen. It connected six rooms in total, or to the same dining room, though the kitchen had two storage rooms that had the same finite magic applied to the bins back at Camp. None of the rooms bore any insignia that labeled them as either the room for the steaming pool, the guards' armory, bathrooms, showers, frigidarium, and the room where only the government officials have access to the Impregnating River—the others were just on the water well that was somewhat guarded in case of someone of any status within the city tried to commit underage [BLEEP].

But we struck out like sore thumbs against all the residents within the palace. Like, The Xiliangs wore modest clothing, but we were roughly wearing the kind of clothing that would be considered the same modest clothing more than three hundred years after the style died out.

"Welcome our guests, Garcia, Quanfei, and Yue." Zolàna announced to the rest of the officials, "These were the three that had journeyed here."

The officials themselves weren't exactly happy for me, but they never dared to touch me other than Garcia and Yue. They all looked at me like my first stepmother did when I got a literal B on the first test I ever took—and even when I am eleven years old, it's just normal for me. Only out of the fifteen officials, one of them was the oldest, but respectfully had my privacy taken into mind.

Seating wasn't assigned unless one was an official, and since we sat on a rectangular table with Zolàna's seat right at the front, the rest were very canted to allow an even number of seats, with ours not labeled with our names but raised by wooden slabs since of our height difference. I sat right between Zolàna and the eldest official, while Yue, Elizabeth, and Garcia sat on the opposite end, directly across from me.

The table itself was very practical, with multiple square platforms going all the way around the table on a rail system, though they all were confined to three-fifths of the table's width and fifteen-seventeenths of the length. Three trays would be directly in front of Zolàna, while at the other end, there was just enough space for an extra tray to be installed. The entire system was quite complex, though one-fifth of its width was roughly equivalent to the citizens of the Xiliang's arm stretching as far out as possible without leaving the seat that was pushed into the smallest comfortable clearance between the table and the body.

"Gracious, the queen allowed a man inside this holy site." One of them muttered, "That [BLEEP] of the world."

"I heard that." Zolàna hissed, "Do you want to respect the new world of that they oust in which even the slightest girl with short hair just 'cause? Plus, you disrespected our oldest one here at 104 years of age-as well as Zhu Bajie, the occasional visitor here ever since 1911."

"Sorry, Your Majesty." The same one sat down and waited for the breakfast to come in.

"As the Homeland Operations department's administrator." the oldest of the officials began to speak, "I hereby suspend you of your duties until that 1914 brain of yours changes for the better, and off, off you shall go with none of your money."

The one official protested, but when the guards at each four corners of the room took two steps toward her, she relented and left with a huff.

"Sorry for the inconvenience," the elder said to me, "Some of us haven't changed ever since the first *recorded* leader's heartbreak."

"It's fine," I said.

With that, the breakfast for every official and side dishes came steaming in, albeit at a moderate pace as it included hot soups that would've caused harm. I was already familiar with most of them, and in the order of the serving subdivision by the serving order, there were: chow mien, lamian, lo mien, biangbiang noodles, lemon rice, fried rice, regular rice, braised pork belly, century eggs, soy eggs, tea eggs, pickled cabbage, baozi, zongzi, congee, crispy fried chicken (the kind that is poached, dried, then deep fried with a result *not* like Popeye or KFC's variant), red bean soup, wonton noodles, zhaliang, hot-dry noodles, chicken feet, and clean pig intestines (chopped to 1-centimeter slices)—no dogs, cats, bats, or snakes were on the menu.

We all used chopsticks as the only sort of silverware that we could even use as there were no knives, forks, spoons, or even sporks set for every plate in front of every seat. At least the only beverage options we had were tea, water, or rice wine, so don't get the perception that all Asians like tea and tea only as we have some who'd prefer the wine.

"Cheers." Zolàna held up her wineglass, "Chaos is mostly subdued back at Camp!"

"To the people!" the entire table stood and raised their cups.

At roughly the same time Zolàna sat back down, the dining began.

"So,did anything happen on the journey?" Zolàna asked us as we ate, "Other than the killing."

Garcia, Yue, and I told her the entire story: from the moment the plane crashed to the moment we entered this very city. Every detail, including that one of the strangest anomalies, we spotted not far from here.

"Interesting." Elizabeth said, "That far and you made it."

"Since you're the only male here Hui…" Zolàna forked an zhaliang, "My grandmother could've saw you if she didn't pass away just five years ago."

"Don't eat that." Garcia said out of the blue.

"What?" I asked, "This is—"

"I'm talking to your Majesty."

"This piece of food?" Zolàna asked, "It's not poisonous."

"I just had the gut feeling it is."

The entire table silenced fro an moment, but resumed as if it wasn't important.

"Quan, can you test it with your… flame?" Garcia asked.

With just one finger, I summoned an fire that danced just to the edge of the fingertip—not like an candle, but one that was hot, colorless, odorless, and smokeless like a Bunsen burner. Sure it was thinner than it was tall, but since it was completely colorless and had an core temperature 100 degrees hotter than a traditional candle, I had to be careful of starting a fire.

"So should I hold it over the fire of someone's finger?" Zolàna asked Garcia, "Why? In all these years?"

"Kings and queens would have the tendency of getting assassinated due to the minority's hatred." I answered, "Some live an long life but death the haters deliver would at times seep through since wealth is normally translated to having power."

"Okay, then I trust you with your history." Zolàna said and just slowly put the piece of food just inches above the flame.

The portion of my own fire that was from the layer where the flame met the zhaliang flared in several colors that seemed very similar, but it somehow rang alarm bells about its compounds as I even wafted the smell towards me, just in tiny amounts.

If I was an actual dog, I would've immediately set the alarms off for the guards acting as security as the compounds *hidden* within had an notion that a *Echinococcus multilocularis* was co-inhabiting the zhaliang with a horde of other compounds that in an modern world, would originate from an artificial intelligence that was designed for finding new medicines for illnesses.

"Your majesty...." I began, "This... is not safe as it contains lead, mercury, and plaster."

Like an volcano that had an boulder blocking its caldera for centuries, Zolàna stood and screamed out at the top of her lungs in anger, "WHO DID THREATEN THE QUEEN?!"

That tone just swept over everyone in the room like another Mount Saint Helen eruption, silencing officials completely.

"It was not me sir." a servant said off to the left, "I did not plan for it."

"Fingers, please." the eldest official ordered.

The servant slowly set the cup he was holding on the table and revealed her hands. The hands were clear of anything, though what would be the relative to the guard-and-door questions, the elder asked, "If I asked you is it unsafe for your hands to touch the silvers of the treasury room, would you say yes?"

"Yes." the servant answered as soon as the question ended.

"Did you say yes?"

"No, I didn't." the servant awaited further questions.

Zolàna silently drew an straight line across her neck with her finger, and hissed, "I'll make you shorter by a head."

Off the servant went to the chopping block.

Soon, breakfast was over, with every last chunk of solid food gone down the stomachs of every official other than the piece of zhaliang that was particularly infected.

"So… " Zolàna got off of her seat as the cleaning division of servants arrived, "How was the dinner?"

"Great." I said, "The food weren't so bad, but no need to thank me for the detecting the traitor."

"Yeah, thank you." Zolàna said, "Are you even a fighter?"

"Demigods at Camp are trained to be as well as to be brainy." Yue answered.

"WHAT DID YOU SAY?!" a angry female voice shouted from behind us.

I turned around and there was just this one royal guard standing and with her guandao bearing in an stance that would intimidate others.

"Head of the royal guard division of the city's defense system." Mallory sighed, "Can one day pass without the extremes?"

"I WILL NOT ALLOW AN MALE TO PASS THE GATES!"

"He has the permit that my grandmother made specifically

for this situation." Zolàna muttered under her breath, "Triss, how about that—"

"Net—it's expired!" Triss shouted just jabbing her glaive as if to threaten her subordinate, "She died, so it doesn't count!"

"Then what do you want?!" Zolàna snapped.

"Death to that [BLEEP]!" Triss was fuming by now, "One on one fight—no warm-up!"

The immediate mood was absolutely silent as the guards that were around other than the four of us had barely negotiated an truce, though as far as I could confirm with my dream, I had the right to stay, but it just seemed harder with an person who could have been reincarnated as an bull who never knows the mediocre balance between peace and discord.

"Has she always been like this?" I whispered.

"Yes, you could've seen it when she saw her first banana." Mallory silently answered.

"I just have an one hit obliterator."

Mallory did not respond.

"Okay, fair and square." I raised my voice towards Triss, "To the death."

.

We ended up in the testing coliseum of the guards' quarters.

Yes, it was totally underground with only three entryways—one for the audience and the rest was for the fighters to enter through. The walls were just as high, with even the seats being directly behind an wall that highly would be an hotspot for suicide, and the arena itself was faceted into eight regions: with only half of those reserved for the onlookers who wanted to see the results. With the walls sort of slanted outwards, the playing field—even when I got there—was soaked in blood, though dried through the years. Light mostly came from the glow stones that were located in niches etched into the support pillars, so the room remained pretty dark—but bright enough to just make outlines of which is where, though the chandelier was directly above the center, wrought with iron and bronze with possibly no candles.

Due to Triss' unstable nature, Mallory was forced behind her back to be the starting referee—standing at the closest row out of all of the seating while others got to sit.

"The game… will start in four minutes." Mallory announced with an shaky undertone, "Triss versus the male."

I could already tell the Mallory just wanted some peace for she is more of an mediator, but Triss was like the bull full of pride in her training to something that once used to be an trap to kill anything—even gods, though it was disarmed by an mortal before it could even strike in a way similar to how the modern bomb disposal squad does for an improvised explosive device.

"Three minutes remaining." Mallory said after a while.

Triss and I both hefted our weapons.

"This is so much like the Hunger games in my dream." I muttered.

"Well, you [BLEEP], there will be no males allowed like the law in 1710." Triss said.

"Two minutes."

This was about the approximate time when we started strafing the center counterclockwise. With the opponent being slightly a bit larger than me as well as in strength, I had a bit of an advantage in relative weights as not all thing heavy an large are as effective as something more like a colony of mice.

"One minute… get ready."

Triss immediately charged, and since Mallory didn't even giver the signal, the royal guard forfeited her own patience for the gold.

"QUANFEI!" Yue shouted to me just as she swung the guandao with more brute force, going at level with my internal squishy pink organ. I ducked under when it was a foot away, sidestepped in the opposite direction, and with the seemingly innocuous wristband I had, guarded steps as one of the worst case scenarios would be that I lost the mobility to move without any hindrance early in the death match.

Triss then rocked on the balls of her feet and tried to gut me straight through the rectum, but was discouraged when it hit my shield, shattering just a tiny piece of the tip off like a boulder that mostly consisted of soapstone.

"You little runt." Triss cursed.

"Too much pride, I tell you." I said.

Sidestepping once more, she barely just managed to plunge the blade into my spine, though I immediately swung my shield to face her in the nick of time that she was not even fazed by such an move, going off to my left and for once, I managed to follow.

Waiting for an strike. I heard Yue's thoughts, *Release your guard and dodge.*

The moment I let my arm droop, Triss followed up with an sweep at my knees which I had been half-anticipating. I jumped in the nick of time, when the adrenaline kicked in, ignoring my limits and going shield-less with just a pen.

Triss was fast as thunder of course, but I might as well been as fast as light. The moment when I aimed for the waist, Triss used her own guandao to block my swing, leveraging it out of her way and defensively intimidating me to back off onto an wall.

"You'd better." Triss aggressively taunted.

I then raised my shield just in time for Triss to injure her knee. In the following second, Triss tried to ram the butt of her glaive to my forehead, but it completely shattered, resulting in a loss for her but with an fighting spirit, continued to her last breath.

"You wanna see light?" I hissed.

"You'll never see it again."

With just the wall behind and death in front, I willed an bright flame to appear and burn just when Triss punched my guts. It was probably too bright, but I fired it off like an electromagnetic rail cannon straight to the chandelier, setting the whole thing quickly ablaze—too hot that the rope that hung it for ages snapped, slamming into the ground with an mass heavy enough to crack the floor.

"AH!" Triss herself bent over in a seizure, "Hundun—Great God! Please! No!"

Hundun? Yue thought in my head, *Who is even that?*

"YOU FOOL!" Triss slammed her head like her corrupted side was leaving her.

I took Triss by one arm as her seizure was getting worse, and pulled her up as the flames quickly raced past the competitors' gates, though never getting further as the floor beyond the halfway point was made of inflammable materials.

It totally did not have candles, though the ground soon began to crumble.

Triss definitely did enter the comatose stage at this point, falling limp as if to reboot herself. I would say I wasn't alone as Yue helped me put Triss over the barrier that laid between us while I had to do the same painstaking process myself.

At around the same time I set my final foot over the barrier, the ground far below heaved in a sigh, and just crumbled, leaving an chasm that stretched for miles below into the abysmal darkness. I watched the latter happen, though Zolàna was the one watching most of it happen.

It wasn't the dark that worried me… though it was of the splotch of the same substance most of us—other than the queen of the Xiliang Nation—had seen, with the same texture and coloration, though it slunk away as soon as I set my eyes upon it.

"To be as polite…" Mallory began, "I've never seen that goo… anywhere."

"Me… neither." Elizabeth slithered around Zolàna's neck as a regular python, "There is no such thing in the world as active as that thing."

"Let's not go there." I said, "It may—"

"Order…" Zolàna raised an finger, "Quanfei, Garcia and Yue, go down there and see where the tunnel leads."

"Okay… why?" Yue asked, "After Quanfei had risked his life a moment ago?"

"It's an exploratory." Zolàna answered, "We'll be waiting here."

Echoes

With nothing but hands, feet, and our abilities we carefully descended into the forgone chasm.

Well, Garcia had to have an piggyback ride one Yue as she skipped in the seemingly dry air, making tiny but phenomenal steps that slowly descended. I went alone after Yue was clear of any collateral damage that could be possible, using both my hands to slowly descend downwards, the flames blasting away like the 1969 lander. Not a single error did I ever allow, though I had to at multiple instances, quickly adjust to accommodate the shakiness that I had like some sportsman trying parallel bars in gymnastics for the very first time.

"Ceiling collapsed under iron." Yue wondered aloud, "Where there's an basement... or not."

"Slow." I gripped Garcia's wrist as soon as she took an single misstep among the rubble, "Don't want to fall into another basement, wouldn't you?"

"Yeah…" Garcia's voice almost echoed.

I and Yue took an deep scan from our positions around, Garcia carefully placing her feet wherever there was solid ground.

The area itself was old—cobwebs and dust-style old. Taken in the fact that the chandelier broke the ceiling, there were broken support pillars with pieces of the ceiling itself strewn everywhere. Every single thing could be dated to pre-1945: the wires that weren't there, the morse code tapping device, and various other stuff. I could hint of mustard gas once being here, but this… was entirely an different world from where the city where it stood in its shadows for almost 50 years.

Directly in front of us, was of the room where echoes of hungry ghosts could be heard—-and by the noise level and the patterns… they weren't too happy or friendly. That very room had an plaque over to its left that read:

HAPPY GHOSTS—YOUR FAVORITE GHOSTS ARE OUT!
* Li-gui's () are the best at growing crops.
* Gudu-gui's () are the friendliest of them all!
* Bagui's () the best at bringing fresh rains.
* Wangliang-gui's () the prettiest of them five!
* AND… Yanggui's () are the best of dreams!

That… I knew was pure irony and hyperbole: the sing lists of the *five* most deadliest ghost types, and just a flip of the meanings would tell you what they were actually.

An ninety degrees turn clockwise from that, there was this massive hall with an flight of stairs that stretched down with no end in sight. Darkness bathed of the emptiness like it was its realm without bright.

Directly behind us was of the trial of goop that belonged to the entity, somehow it had left it there on purpose, though whatever laid between—life or death… it was seemingly hinting of which way was which.

"Should we follow the trail?" I asked Yue and Garcia.

"Since Mallory asked us to investigate, then sure we could." Garcia answered.

Yue nodded, and just when anomalies couldn't get used to

taking an break, an deep voice echoed, "FOUR… FOUR… FOUR… THREE-THREE… THREE… NINE-NINE-NINE-SIX… SIX-SIX… EIGHT-EIGHT…"

"What was that?" Yue asked as soon as the echoes were over.

"If you…" I tried to interpret it.

We were silent in an unanimous agreement of eyes that I should keep my fire, though with my left hand burning while I hand my right on the unsheathed pufengdao. Step by step, we went inside.

Our steps echoed in the tunnel, my fire as right as possible to light up all immediate sides as we descended.

Just two miles from where we started, we came into an room—an vast room, full of nothing on the floor… but an myriad ghosts who bear no origin other than the very gender as female—all of them, hanging from ceilings as women in their 20s or older upon invisible string like they were hanged—several of them dating back to the time of when entire families all the way down to the oldest ones living were killed just cause one broke the law.

"Ba Jiao Gui's" Yue said in awe, "This is going to be worse."

The next room we explored was a floor down, a room where it split into three halls that were abandoned: one by my mental radar was blocked someplace deep in the dark, another was a former bridge now broken off, but the other one… it was highly cognito-hazardous for some reason with mirages of monsters that I knew from the back of my hand that they were Chinese entities. I dare not to describe them, but they all were deadly in their own ways.

"We know, you are there!" Yue shouted, "Come up and reveal yourselves!"

My wristband immediately fired three quick pulses before

expanding itself, snaking around my arms, wrapping around my torso, almost autonomously covering every vital inch of the body before I was left with wearing armor: the same Damascus-like appearance as my weapon.

"NINE… THIRTEEN… FIVE… ONE…" an voice boomed from the strange corridor.

I checked myself, just to make sure that the "gift" was not a joke, scanning everywhere that I could see but seeing no joke features or impracticalities: I was wearing plated armor that had an much darker overall shade than my saber, sectioned in plates in the style of the Tang Dynasty's, though with improvements such as sealed crevices, lighter weight, exoskeletal frame, an face mask, a visor, and modules that were of key importance such as an 360° sonar, radar, rangefinder, and night vision.

"THIRTEEN… THIRTEEN…" the same voice echoed, "NINE… ONE… THREE…"

"DARE TO COME OUT!" Garcia shouted in fright.

The next moment, I saw it slowly creep out.

Initially I thought I was hallucinating when its front-right leg came out as an scorpion's tendon, but the next one on the left told me it wasn't, emerging slowly out of the shadows like an human's hand that had been severely starved and elongated. Both were eerily inky black with an blue hue, though it kept repeating as it revealed its… collarbone section. It did not even have an face, or the seven holes one needed to sense its surroundings.

Then emerged its torso, with mismatching wings as well as legs, though for the wings, they came in only pairs in the mentioned order: dragonfly, bee, and a falcon's wings. There were additional noise other than the chant though, most of it coming from the insectoid wings vibrating at an pace unmatched.

"THIRTEEN…" it began to chant like it was an madman, "THIRTEEN…"

"WTF." Yue spoke.

I looked at Yue and she mouthed an entirely different sentence.

The next moment, it froze in place, but its stomach brutally compressed like it was taking an bleeper, but the thing it puked out… let's say it was an old preserved *human* skeleton, complete with the uniform that Camp possibly had before I was here.

"IF YOU…" the anomaly began a new loop.

With the humanoid appendage, it began slowly reaching out, the acidic goo it was made of dripping like venom, hissing and being somehow inversely heated that the air immediately around the droplets began to heat up to desert-like conditions.

"Hundun…" Yue now sounded happy.

"Yes, sorry for killing you, Fred…" Garcia was unfortunately affected by the presence.

I quickly closed the distance the next second, moving as fast as I could while having the sword prepared to strike.

"DARE—" Hundun monotonously droned on.

I struck at the moment, the sound of the Bing steel cleaving through the goop making an noise very similar to some semi-viscous magma that was also highly reactive to air, bursting into flames that only lasted about one second, trailing behind the false edge like wakes behind a boat.

Was it the machine or my fault at what happened next? I still don't know as the moment the stroke was done, the armor I had on shrunk back into the same old wristband. Not to two-time myself, Hundun opened its mouth wider than its supposed head, revealing rows and rows of teeth angled inwards like an anglerfish, but with that same abysmal darkness that the taotie had.

The sound was low and loud like an bass or semi-muted thunder, but at the exact event mark, I was flooded with… just unspeakable items.

In the first second, it was notably the Ragnarok event of the Norsemen legends. The tree that was somehow an relative to the one I had in one of my dreams was definitely by the myth of such, but it had one key difference: there wasn't an renewal like the myth had said there would. The event as by Hundun's projection was to be like the Big Chill phase for the end of the current universe.

The following five seconds, it was recursively more cramped with happy accidents.

But by the time it ended, Hundun was gone from sight, my mind and those who witnessed the god-demon almost shattered like glass.

"YAAAAAA!"

That… that didn't need any introduction with a thousand million voices screaming the same at the tunnel we did not travel through. Those were more likely the ghosts of the Japanese ranging from the ones who were in deployment in 1937 to the ones indoctrinated in 1944 or so. Not an ancient form of an Chinese ghost, but much deadlier in a sense that they had rifles, though there might be denial whether it 's true or not nowadays for either country.

The opponent was ruthless as always in their life before death. Every one of them was an infantryman, formerly serving the top brass like madmen who only knew of their own country. Their ghosts, however, still never slept for they had no way of hearing directly from the world of the living that the war was over—

only their descendants that at least lived past the surrender ever accepted only after another weapon was deployed to kill with a thousand golden crows, though at an perquisite cost that possibly certain branches of the family line being held within camps.

But to survive… we truly did fight.

Each ghost disappeared under the mild injuries we inflicted like as if the metal that our weapons were made of could even interact with the metaphysical realm of the dead.

But how I wish I was one of them, as the moment I killed my last ghost of the day, the effects of such adrenaline and the anomaly came into effect with one last split-second flash of the worst illogical scenarios.

As if it had adapted after just minutes of fighting, my nerves' nodes went full overdrive, sensing every death of any of my scenarios that it just seemed way too real and bloody. I would not even dare to speak of them, but all I could tell you: it's not as the same as any horror film tropes.

"Quanfei!" Yue exclaimed as I stumbled with no definite direction.

"Quan?" Garcia asked Yue.

"I'm not fine." I began to curve in an s-shaped pattern.

"Are you sure?"

"No, I'm definitely not." my head incessantly throbbed like an bulbous explosion just happened, "I may have some… slightly severe eating disorder."

"Hurry—he's—"

I missed two of the many steps of the stairs that once had the Japanese ghosts, and fell, hitting my head every three steps or so so hard that by the time I was about three-quarters of the way there, I completely blacked out.

Burnout

"Wait. those colors..." Elizabeth said, "That color... it was the same faceless guy."

"What?" Garcia asked, "It's a living object?"

"Yes, I was swimming underwater when that diver without eyes guided me to a cave." Elizabeth said, "I thought it was safe."

"If two entities of similar properties had existed at two places..." Yue muttered, "It's the deadliest."

Like a tidal wave, the entire dining table fell silent and turned towards us as if they had heard what Yue had said. Happiness was now completely gone, washed away like the long-forgotten birthday of a human.

"How?" Zolàna asked Yue, "How can it be?"

"That's what we call the Chaos." Elizabeth began to warm up: "The monster that can exist in multiple places at once Not everyone can detect it; not everyone can see it, but it's just *there*."

"Go on," Zolàna politely ordered. "There would be more to it."

"Due to the ambiguity of bad, there's no way of catching it in its true form as it bears no identifying shape. The most invisible among mortals, it's also the god of what it represents as to be evil—and to speak of it as the Highest Lord is wrong, and nay, nor do I say its name since its thousand times more endless than the gods combined, more deadly than some giant [BLEEP] robot that threatens to devour planets and stars—the equivalent of the Greek form of Chaos that is unbound by any sort of chains to Diyu—or Chinese hell."

"How do you even know this much information?" Yue asked Elizabeth.

"My mother warned me of it."

That pressed the big red no-no button inside everyone who had heard it. Every one of the officials left and went to their offices like this was six minutes before a hydrogen bomb exploded right over their heads or bats out of hell. Horns on all watchtowers soon sounded the pattern of an increase in defense within five minutes of the last official leaving the very room.

"Any additional info?"

"The best times for it to rise is the pandemics, extreme natural disasters, worst economic depressions, great famines, and the pure world at war." Elizabeth answered, "According to my mother, that is since she is immortal."

"We must prepare," Zolàna looked around the room, "Servants, execute operation Curtains Down. This is not a drill."

"What's that even supposed to mean?" I asked.

"It's just from my grandmother's SOS cookbook." Zolàna replied, "We need to hit the wagon."

"Yes, majesty." Yue took hold of my hand, "It's urgent."

"Remind me to say this to the Monkey King," Zolàna requested, "In case I forget, it's telling him to execute."

"What?" Garcia and I chimed in.

"Execute Protocol 13. No words to be said. Let's get on with it—bring my bodyguard with me!"

IV

Triparté

If one does time travel, attempts will at the best conditions skips into the future for that thing of which to time travel only slows down the time within while to the one inside the vehicle would the outside time seem to stretch, thus making the dear traveler an time capsule to the old days before it ever lands since the time outside will be greater than the time projected inside—with time traveling back being reality-breaking as it could create paradoxes.

Thunderbold

"We are the ones who delivered the horse."

That was said by an Insurgent-tier OFT member who was at the Nevada-Utah border with his cronies by his side. Yes, it's dead of the night—but don't expect clear skies. Even when I look up into the skies, where stars should've been showing up as diamonds, an entire thick cloud of sorts blocks out everything other than fogging up the moon itself. Zolàna was getting some shut-eye in the wagon, besides Triss, who was still comatose. Elizabeth was sleeping under Garcia's sleeping spot within the same wagon, while Yue was beside me, holding the bright lantern upon her lap.

The insurgent himself was wearing his full Order of the Faceless uniform, complete with a full-face mask that hid his identity. Dressed in a gruesome color of black and purple with an improvised armor set that consisted of ferromagnetic metals that are found in everyday objects, it was rather like another day to cause chaos—equipped with a crossbow and a quiver full of iron rods as long as the draw length.

"No, we are the ones," Yue said to them. "The horse is already in its stable."

"Fred is the staunch champion, you fame-stealer," the Insurgent said. "He journeyed to Virginia to have that."

"Who is it then?" I asked him, "Who is it to be the Good God that is on your side?"

"Hundun, the Faceless One."

The tone in which he said it consisted exactly of no mercy.

"The Jade—" Yue began.

"Don't say that name—blasphemy will it be?" The insurgent loaded his crossbow and pointed it at Yue's face. "Say that again, and you'll be sorry."

To keep him distracted, I mentally sent that message to Yue.

"Well, okay," Yue said, "I submit."

"Sure," the crossbow was raised to point directly at the forehead, "Say that again."

"I'll give you my bank account, but first, I need to turn off this lamp in case the resistor is frayed."

Yue, with a mask of calmness, turned off the very light that lit the way back home.

"What?" the insurgent said after a moment. "Where are you guys?"

Oops. Yue thought in my head.

Do we need to fight in the dark? I asked the mental version of Yue.

I am of water abilities, but you are the counter to wood, and metal. Yue answered.

I then began slowly heating my hands up, rather covering my palms as they began to glow, but rather to let it out, I awaited the Insurgent's next move in the playacting playacting.

"Crows of the OFT—search!" the insurgent commanded, "They have disappeared!"

The next moment, they were met with fire engulfing them as quickly as striking an match, it in itself billowing out at 900 yards while I controlled it with my two hands cupped more like autonomous adjustable vectoring nozzle. They died of no sound, but at least Yue cleaned the area with her water abilities.

"The fourth time you used your abilities," Yue smiled and said, "Great job, but can I hold your hand for the rest of the trip?"

"Yes," I said, "I'll have to use my left."

"No worries," Yue said, turning the lantern back on. "I'll grab the other rein, and we'll be equal."

* * *

The situation back at Camp Quite was not another civil war.

"So this is what you'd call home." Zolàna said as we passed through the main gates, "An entire city-state halfway across the US."

"Yes, and it houses roughly more than just a hundred residents." I said, "Given any time, it only houses six generations, for the seventh usually leaves."

"Oh, so where are those gang members?" Triss asked, "I just woke up and… I'm sorry, I was very proud of myself."

I, Yue, or Garcia didn't have to answer them as we got to the plaza right in front of the library, with an entire crowd paving the way for the Xiliang Nation's queen to move through. What they were surrounding was an execution of thousands of OFT partisans.

"Why that execution?" Garcia asked me, "Why not something more humane?"

"China in the earliest days was a bit trippy." I answered, "One mistake that affected even the local government, and the whole family's going down the drain."

Zolàna hopped off, with Triss following suit, and with Sun Wukong near the guillotine, she signaled for him for a brief chat. Even if I am eleven years old, I would not go full force against them, though I will not recite the entire conversation for Zolàna's sake. At least Triss would be by her side at such public events, putting up an air of death that pretty much deterred all of the others from getting close to Zolàna.

While they were doing so, the infamous paparazzi came into the scene which could be a once-in-a-lifetime opportunity as Zolàna stood out like a speck of black against a light gray background. They had the flash on, so each time the trigger was pressed, I had to close my eyes and thus; I did hate them as they could've used the natural light instead since it was a day where the sun shone with very few clouds.

That also reminds me of the moment not far in the past when passengers in black boxes were never helped but were left to die, like the one in an enclosed street somewhere. Do they even know how serious it is to chase after them? Or are they going internally for the money *per* picture instead of *either* the instinct to rescue the moment disaster happens or the thought of needing some days off for the subject? They might as well install thousands of cameras everywhere just to call it "not invading privacy", with immediate stories that may as well be so focused on pathos that there's no room for ethos or logos.

"I just hate those flashy thingies." Elizabeth slowly crawled over my shoulder and said, "In the middle of the flippin' daytime."

"If I were the head of Camp, then I would've banned them from doing this." I said, "I am particularly sensitive to lights such as these. Tracking media, I could have suggested an permanent ban with death from a squad as the immediate consequence."

"Sure, but wouldn't that be too harsh?"

"No, not too harsh." I replied, "The media can have all they want, but these days… from 2014 to 2018…"

"Yeah, ordinary people getting tracked other than from the Federal Bureau of Investigation and the Central Intelligence Agency… the world may as well be so thirst of personal knowledge of others that it is an complete incurable paranoia of what George Orwell or even Lois Lowry did not want." Elizabeth glanced at Zolàna, "Even if it sounds like the old legalism's view of that if death was for the smallest infractions, there can be much worse consequences."

With a simple release of the ropes to the very guillotine, every single one of us fell silent. The first was a male criminal who was the Senator—a position similar to student body representatives—of condominiums in sector 1. It was a rather ghastly sight. They pulled the blade up, the body was disposed of, and the next victim was a female who—if I remember correctly—was the representative for sector two's street maintenance.

In a moment, the ringleader—the main Insurgent who held the position of a waiter for a café—was killed and diced into thousands of pieces.

"This is inhumane… But since I don't want to have another civil war, I'll allow it," Garcia said to Yue.

"Yes, I don't either," Yue said.

"So… I've got my room now." Zolàna showed us her room key: "It's 8-15-305."

"That's right next to us." I and Garcia somehow perfectly timed it.

We both glanced at each other, and just by the looks of it, we seemed to not know who said it first.

"I said it first." We somehow said the same thing within milliseconds of each other.

"How did you guys manage that?" Zolàna asked Garcia, "Is it scripted?"

"No." we both answered at the same time.

As if Zolàna remembered such a joke, she began to smile for what was probably the brightest smile ever since leaving the city back at the Xiliang Nation. She was an adult, and with the conversation between Sun Wukong and her, she was free to mostly enjoy a civilian life instead of some variant equivalent to a slightly de-powered King Charles the First of England.

"Then how can you time it so well?"

"We don't." Yue joined in the conversation.

"Oh, then it happens by chance," Zolàna said, "Just so you know."

"Okay…" I said.

"Then who does live near me?" Zolàna asked us.

"We're neighbors." Yue and Garcia said

"So… let me get this straight… Yue, Garcia, and Quanfei live in separate rooms, and they are neighbors to each other, with mine being right next to all of yours. does that mean… Do I just live between either of you?"

"I and Quanfei live as roommates," Yue said to Zolàna. "So it's either my room or Garcia's."

"So… I am living right next to Yue's," Zolàna said, "With just a few young friends of mine."

"How did you figure it out?" Garcia asked.

Elizabeth, who was previously upon my shoulder, appeared over Zolàna's left shoulder, smiling as she dangled those keys that were to our rooms upon the tip of her tail.

"Your keys are here." Elizabeth jokingly taunted.

"Could we have our keys back?" I asked Elizabeth.

"Sure thing."

"Camp seems a bit different from what my grandma told me of." Zolàna questioned, "Could I explore while Camp is still the peacetime version of itself?"

"Yes, whenever you'd like."

"How about your keys?" Elizabeth was somehow a bit further away. "Catch me if you can."

Black Lights

The days at Camp were—by the trend line of how busy they were on average—mostly numbered.

I don't mean they dropped to zero, but it came and went more like an ocean wave—they'd go to other schools during the fall and spring to not raise any suspicions of being dead from whatever sort of chaser or disease. Summer quickly passed with Zolàna and Triss immediately crunching down their skills to the point that they would, by a wide margin, almost always occupy either a medical surgeon or psychiatrist position within any such service group, and by the time we knew it, it was just six weeks before August 8th of 2018.

That was very much the last day of packed meal service locations, and it meant that those locations had the day to make lower prices without aiming for more profit in the sense that real-world colleges would make one pay for the education, and thus the closest there was to be was more like the top-10 rewards system that gave out legitimate cash only to those above 9th grade and still in school, though they will blacklist those who do fall into heavy debt or bankruptcy even *once*.

"We have come so far; for the year 2018, we have four months to pass the flame onto the new year." Sun Wukong broadcasted his annual speech: "This has been a tremendous year for all of you within the borders of Camp. With our first four new Residents of this year having done the deed that the grandmother of Zolàna had wished for us to do,"

Zolàna slowly walked out of the diner towards the outdoor public phone booth, right as the first line had rolled off Sun Wukong's tongue.

Cheers erupted around the diner, and we were just glad we somehow stuck together, with Zolàna now having the expertise in psychology to be a full-time worker with an alter-ego of a Taoist magician, while Triss was more like a medical staff member who knew all the body parts of a human from the back of her hand.

"Now comes the end of summer." Sun Wukong let out a sigh. "For kids and children around here, please be respectful of your parents unless at the moment they threaten to maim their only hope of continuing the lineage."

"We did it," Yue whispered in my ear.

"Yeah, we did."

"But be prepared for flybys of these specimens that appeared a day before the minor event known as Skyfall." Sun Wukong continued, "May the good ones of Camp have good luck and high wealth, and the rotten ones fall from the skies like flies. But be safe from the evil ones, for they are never so bare to intentions—otherwise, have balance in pursuit of scholarly minds."

The broadcast immediately went offline, and the visual media that the diner used during that time resumed almost immediately.

In a moment, Zolàna walked back in, sat in front of me, and announced, "You guys are safe."

"What did you do?" I asked.

"I'm having a safe, non-hectic process of transferring your current stepparents to me." Zolàna answered, "They agreed that it might be too much of a hassle to keep losing you guys to disasters, so their lawyers are in a few minutes moving the legal papers to transfer their guardianship to me."

"Just make sure you don't dare to starve my… um…." Yue just couldn't get the word out.

"Yeah, don't starve him or say anything about his body type."

In a matter of two weeks, the transfer from our parents to Zolàna was an absolute success, though we still got to sleep in our rooms in the same condominium. There are no clear skies for the nights, though, even if movies try to say every night is clear; it's foggy as hell.

On August 1st, we had the annual non-celebratory health check for residents of Camp who are not 19 years old or older, meaning that we had our official height checked as well as our eyesight for the upcoming 2018-2019 school year. I passed most of it, though, except for the eyesight, for which I had fresh glasses in contrast to Yue, leave alone Garcia.

Zolàna exceeded expectations of what was to be like a homo sapiens with natural strength comparable to the closest possible to a silverback's brawn and ninety times more brain capacity in terms of how many estimated bytes of storage it has. For Zolàna, her eyesight was tested to have a visual acuity that scored a 20 over two millionths—she could see something ten million times sharper or farther than a regular and pure mortal with 20-20 vision, as well as with her bodyguard having similar medical results.

"Good JOB!" the examiner shouted through the microphone far away. "YOU HAVE PASSED!"

Then came grade-level SAT-standard tests, which Zolàna

didn't need to take as she was now a legal adult, though they remained optional for her as, within the US, one can expect to be somewhere in their 20s or 30s by the time they obtain a PhD.

With the tests being almost equivalent to the gaokao back in China with some influence from the SAT or ACT exams in the US, every stroke, every single space, and every oral exam counted towards the maximum of 750 points. One stroke was wrong, and there goes the point—retakes aren't even allowed.

During the exam, though, we were spaced so far apart and with privacy screens upon the desks that anyone who tried to peek at others' answers was very obvious to the examiner or the classroom's teacher—with electronic receivers at hidden areas of the classrooms just to fish out anyone using devices such as phones, tablets, and even headphones of any kind.

"Do not cheat." The baize lion said a minute before we even began, "This will determine your wit of scholarly practices, as all brawn will not even win against the one that almost all brains possess. "

With the given information, I tried my best, with the teachers sitting there just watching the monitor they had that had cameras facing our backs—yes, it's that tough with those things trying to fish out cheaters. Plus, we had to do it within three days of starting the test as a class.

I remember that first feeling that I would fail when I watched the city-wide network channel meant for students and their guardians. The program first showed the names of every school within Camp before concentrating more on the respective listings, starting with Pre-Kindergarten before going up the grade levels, each time consistently showing ones who scored at least eighty percent of the test correct, though it got a bit less in terms of list length as one approaches the 20-graders working on their Doctorate of Philosophy degrees—with stalemates eliminated through scrutinizing class behavior so that no bad-behaving students would be too proud.

"This is this year, the year of 2018's score," the anchors announced. "No hard feelings, but it was the best."

The entire graph looked more like they had smoothed it out, with the horizontal axis having the variable "score" while the vertical axis was in increments up to the number of students between each level of education comparatively graphed out. The entire elementary average was better than the middle school average, with them being just barely worse than high schools within the entirety of Camp, while higher education made a way less, yet better, difference than the previous.

I also remember the scene when 15 agonizing minutes passed: Yue was to my left on the bed where Mallory would sleep, Garcia sat in the same room but on Triss' bed directly opposite the room, while the two adults were present, Triss just leaning against the door frame while Mallory read an adult novel in bed.

"Look, Yue, we passed on the 1st and 2nd places." Garcia excitedly said, "We are the top two, with Hui just in 3rd!"

I scanned the list of the top six 6th graders, and for a moment, I thought I wasn't there until Yue pointed to my name on the list.

I had missed the exam with just 748 points total, while Yue had 749, and Garcia was lucky to score first place in her grade.

"The top three," the announcement anchor said, "get one and a quarter worth of one-time-use late passes that only extend the assignment's due date for you by a week later than the due date. We provide a 99% discount on prices for three-quarters of a year to the top three individuals. They also get a buy-one-get-one-free incentive during this time. However, ESCO will cancel the offer if they exhaust their credits."

We broke into cheers as the awards for the first three were announced, though Yue politely silenced us as the anchor continued.

"The next three on the displayed list get a 33% discount in the same condition without the buy-one-get-one-free permit since these have only an expiration set to half of a year with no late passes but half of a semester's worth of time waivers up to 8 hours of the after-hours slotted for the regular sleeping time every day—with something greater assigned on the slip will invalidate the slip itself and thus will result in a little chat. The very last three will get only an 11% discount on the same terms as the middle three, with a set expiration of just a single season."

"Lucky for you guys," Zolàna said as she closed her book, "You probably fall for the zero price effect."

As if the anchor had somehow heard Zolàna, it said, "Marketplaces, please do not go for the zero price effect for its greed. Make sure the ones with the BOGOF incentive truly do pay the price for one, or else we'll mark your stores as vacant and irreversibly sell them to other shopkeepers. To the winners, the discounts are optional, though the expiration date's permanent—your discount will be effective starting the moment you enter camp next year."

"Oh," Triss pulled out five sheets of paper, "These are the forms—just a questionnaire about whether we'll stay."

A brief moment of silence followed, with Yue looking at both Garcia and me as if to try to form a universal agreement at such a crossroads, but I was the one this time to break the silence.

"Yes, I would gladly leave."

"Yes, same with my friend." Yue said, "Garcia?"

"Definitely."

"Good, Elizabeth, Triss, and I have mostly filled out ours, so it would be great if you guys could fill out yours. But are you guys sure you want to leave?"

Now it was a group decision between the three of us.

"So… would Skyfall happen again?" Garcia asked Yue, "We almost died there."

"No, a plane crash is most likely to happen during takeoff and landing." Yue answered, "The FAA always makes new regulatory rules for operation and safety, so there will be less of a chance of each accident."

"It's about one out of 11 million." I said to Garcia, "Don't let the past linger eternally on you, but worry about the present that will become the past as choices stack up, though try not to have envy when choosing them."

"Yeah, I get what you are saying." Garcia said, "Yes, Zolàna, we'll go out."

"Unanimous?" Zolàna asked us.

"Unanimous," we all said at the same time.

Looking back at the entire year, I could say it was quite boring, but even then, there would be just the horizon anyone may look upon—the unreachable destination out of all physical places. One can fly as long as they want to that place of which no one has; another can spend all of his savings; but out of the sea of people of any type, the ones who have the engine to both dive into the darkness for the light and trailblaze new paths may be more valuable than those who follow trends that may as well be fads three or more years in the future.

[RECORD.CUT(2018, PhCQHM, Common Era) RECORD.SAV

This recording has reached the end of the tape.

Afterword

No book in print has ever been perfect the first time every author writes.

This book I have been writing so far is the sole novella that I have worked on since I was ten years old. It initially went way too fast in pacing and was so full of potholes that it was more like every other sentence didn't match the plot or the storyline. In my second year of writing this, I managed to slow down the pace but had to adjust some names, actions, and settings, such as the weather. Their nationalities stayed exactly the same, but in order for it to balance, I sort of rewrote the entire story from square one for the second time.

Of course, 2020 hit me when I was working on my third-year version and I could improve my writing of my novel to be more compact if ever was successful and I had to write sequels for those who wanted them… it had to be:

1) Not too heavy for even the hardcover version.

2) Nearing or within the range of either being considered a novella or novel.

3) Feature concepts/entities from the Ancient Chinese.

4) Provide an alternate timeline for what would happen.

5) Free of errors.

My fourth year was probably approaching what it is now. Almost 70 pages worth of text, balanced logic, and sensible flow, but with a few tweaks, such as the style in which I paced it if ever I was in a reader's shoes and if ever my pen name was really another person. From even my first year, I had stuck to the mythology I grew up with and heard of (mainly Journey to the West), even if I can't write much Chinese rather less to speak Mandarin.

The fifth-year version was nearly 80 pages, much more defined and less redundant to have more clarity. The sixth-year version was much improved, with almost perfect grammar (I am bilingual both fluent in Mandarin and English), a smoothed plot line, and a story structure that was just with almost no potholes as much as my first-year version.

At the same time starting to write this novella, I worked and practiced on cover design, initially going for the complex before compressing it down to the minimal. Most of the versions were on Canvas, though from my seventh year and beyond, I wrote it on Reedsy with only the cover design on Canvas.

The events in my story are not real, but the events that happened from 2007 to 2018 influenced the plot line for the entire 14 chapters—leave for some detours that may as well make the printed versions as heavy as a Calculus textbook. For the same reason, I am no thriller or action-drama writer, as I may as well imply problems so vague that the books' sole purpose is to merely entertain.

But what I have to say is ever-so-simple.

Whenever an author writes fiction, there are always two journeys: the journey of the character(s) of the pages that one day may be flipped and played on the stage of the readers, and the journey of the author herself or himself for the seconds that pass. Every journey has a series of crossroads that one must decide but never go back to in regret—nor does traveling faster than light make the earth spin backward.

I just hope for no war and do not expect chaos to end quickly. I only expect that we will find some way of achieving equilibrium that we can live through the longest, but I plead not guilty to firing the figurative cannons that may have injured some or allowed thunder to rumble overhead. I may not ever rest six feet under, but ever more so than to act than to lull away my will to such actions. Most would say it's the spirit, but I'd say the engine, which is metaphorically neither soul, heart, nor spirit, as the heart would be more of a carefree swing for the soul within the spirit, which is only breathed in the space between both organs, and thus, I do not run on spirit or heart, but the brain without brawn.

Signed,
Q. Dagbjort Huangington

About the Author

I don't know what I am, nor do I know myself for myself to know thyself according to oneself.

You can connect with me on:
🐦 https://twitter.com/qihua_huan41950

www.ingramcontent.com/pod-product-compliance
Lightning Source LLC
Chambersburg PA
CBHW031412150726
47989CB00002B/629